"Let down your hair," he demanded

"What?" said Alexa, and she spun around to find Revil only a pace away, his jacket and tie removed, his shirt undone. He exuded a virile sensuality, to which she felt herself responding against her will.

"Take the combs out of your hair and let it down, Alexa," he instructed in a strangely quiet voice.

"No, please!" she begged.

But Revil snaked one hand around her waist and with the other reached up to whip the combs from her hair. Her tresses tumbled down in soft, silvery waves.

"My God," he breathed. "That air of innocence you project is even stronger when your hair is free." Then he sneered, "But we both know that it's a false image, don't we?"

Alexa recoiled in fear....

if she were honest with herself, she would have to admit

YVONNE WHITTAL, a born dreamer, started scribbling stories at an early age but admits she's glad she didn't have to make her living by writing then. "Otherwise," she says, "I would surely have starved!" After her marriage and the birth of three daughters, she began submitting short stories to publishers. Now she derives great satisfaction from writing full-length books. The characters become part of Yvonne's life in the process, so much so that she almost hates coming to the end of each manuscript and having to say farewell to dear and trusted friends.

Books by Yvonne Whittal

Don't miss any of our special offers. Write to us at the following address for information on our newest releases.

Harlequin Reader Service
901 Fuhrmann Blvd., P.O. Box 1397, Buffalo, NY 14240
Canadian address: P.O. Box 603,
Fort Erie, Ont. L2A 5X3

YVONNE WHITTAL

there is no tomorrow

Harlequin Books

TORONTO • NEW YORK • LONDON
AMSTERDAM • PARIS • SYDNEY • HAMBURG
STOCKHOLM • ATHENS • TOKYO • MILAN

Harlequin Presents first edition October 1988
ISBN 0-373-11118-5

Original hardcover edition published in 1987
by Mills & Boon Limited

CHAPTER ONE

THE atmosphere in Salon Danielle's crowded dressing-room was highly charged. Voices were rising and falling in various degrees of excitement, and intermittent laughter seemed to ease the tension amongst Madame Véronique's girls while they prepared themselves to model the latest Danielle fashions for the coming spring. Madame Véronique had trained her models well—they were professionals—but they all knew that the success of this fashion show could result in Madame Véronique's agency procuring the Bradstone contract to model André Dacre's spring collection.

Bradstone Promotions was the largest company of its kind in the country, and they had been assigned to promote the new spring fashions designed by André Dacre, the South African couturier. The Bradstone contract would mean prestige for Madame Véronique's agency; it was the ultimate goal most modelling agencies aimed at, and Madame Véronique deserved the recognition more than most.

Alexa Drew was applying her make-up in front of one of the many mirrors against the wall. She was a vital part of all the tension and excitement surrounding her, and yet there was something about her that held her apart from the rest of the models. Her silky, ash-blonde hair was piled casually but elegantly on to her head, and it was held in place with combs studded with diamanté which sparkled in the bright overhead lights. Her wide, full mouth was attractively modelled with a promise of passion in the slight upward curl of the upper lip, and violet-blue eyes were fringed unexpectedly with long dark lashes beneath perfectly arched, equally dark eyebrows.

'An extraordinary combination for someone whose skin is almost as pale as her hair,' Madame Véronique had once remarked.

It was not this 'extraordinary combination' of her appearance that Alexa Drew was thinking about while she applied a blusher to her delicate cheekbones. She wanted Madame Véronique to get the Bradstone contract more than anyone else in that dressing-room, but her anxiety had nothing to do with their prowess as models. She had a gnawing suspicion that if Revil Bradstone should discover that Alexa Drew was one of Madame Véronique's models, Madame could forget about acquiring the contract she desired so much. There was always the possibility that Bradstone's youthful chairman might not be in the audience that afternoon, but this was a frail hope when Alexa recalled reports of his active involvement in his company's projects.

Madame Véronique entered the dressing-room, her presence sufficient to silence everyone. A tall and slender woman of sixty-five, she still moved with a youthful grace, and the silver streaks across the temples of her otherwise raven-black hair gave Madame a distinguished, sometimes awesome appearance. She smiled, her brown eyes softening and crinkling at the corners when her glance encompassed them all, and Alexa felt herself strengthened by her mentor's calm, confident appearance.

'This is not the time for a lecture,' Madame announced in her faintly accented voice. 'I know you will excel yourselves this afternoon, and I shall be proud of you.' She raised her glance to the electric clock against the wall. 'You have five minutes. Lucille and Alexa, you are to go on first. Be ready, and for goodness' sake do not forget to smile!'

'Smile!' Lucille Upton squealed softly the minute Madame's back was turned. 'I'm so nervous I'll need all my concentration not to trip over my own feet when I walk out on to that platform, and then I'm still expected to smile!'

Alexa did not answer her while they slipped into the cool and colourful polyester dresses with their matching short-sleeved jackets. She no longer felt the same; professionalism had taken over, and her nervous anxiety had been replaced by a methodical, almost deathly calmness. She checked the dresses on the rack beside her and the neat row of shoes beneath them. There would be no time for fumbling, and Madame would not tolerate errors which could have been avoided with a little care.

Danielle, a small auburn-haired woman, flitted around amongst them, her hands deftly making last minute alterations to her cleverly designed garments. She spoke calmly and smiled often, but occasionally her teeth would bite into her full lower lip as an indication of her own nervousness.

They received the signal. The volume of the music relayed in the salon was toned down to play softly in the background for the duration of the fashion show. It was time to go on.

Alexa held her breath, mentally crossing her fingers while she waited in the wings with Lucille, then they stepped out behind the curtains and, with Madame Véronique's comforting presence behind the microphone, they walked along the low, carpeted platform. They paused midway, remembering to smile as they turned slowly to give the audience a better view all round of Danielle's creations, and they did the same at the end of the platform, removing their jackets and trailing them casually behind them as they retraced their steps to the sound of appreciative murmurs.

The next two models were waiting in the wings. They stepped out into the spotlight the moment Alexa and Lucille disappeared behind the green velvet curtain, and for Alexa the first and worst hurdle had been accomplished with reasonable success.

There was a mad scramble in the dressing-room. The whisper of silk was in Alexa's ears when she slipped into the patterned, low-cut cocktail-dress. Danielle was there to zip Alexa and Lucille into their dresses and to cast a critical eye over their appearance before they exchanged their shoes for gold sandals. Alexa checked her hair and her make-up, and added a darker eyeshadow to tone in with the deep blue of her dress.

Alexa waited in the wings with Lucille for the second time that afternoon, her mind whirling with everything Madame Véronique had taught her, and then they were walking out again on to the low platform, their manner calm and composed, and that all-important smile on their lips.

They reached the end of the platform, and Alexa turned slowly, allowing her impersonal glance to skip across the sea of unfamiliar but appreciative faces. The butterflies in her stomach were beginning to settle down, she had been unnecessarily afraid, but, as fate would have it, her glance collided unexpectedly with cold, unforgettable grey eyes, and the contempt in their depths was clearly visible even at a distance. For one fraction of a second her step faltered, but she regained her composure swiftly, and continued. Revil Bradstone was in the audience, as she had feared he might be. Three years had elapsed since their last, brief meeting, but the coldness and contempt in those smoky grey eyes still had the power to affect Alexa like a physical blow.

He had not forgotten; he would never forget, and neither would he believe her if she was ever given the opportunity to confront him with the truth.

Alexa had Madame Véronique's rigid training to thank for her ability to continue as if nothing disturbing had occurred, but her pulse rate was jerky when the fashion show ended two hours later, and a tiny nerve was jumping erratically at the corner of her softly curving mouth.

'*Mes enfants,* you were all *magnifiques!*' Madame exclaimed, resorting to her native tongue in her excitement as she swept into the dressing-room with her arms outstretched as if to embrace them all. 'I have been talking to Bradstone's public relations officer, and the contract is almost assuredly ours, *but...*' Madame paused for breath, her dark eyes sparkling like jewels. '... we shall be notified of their decision at the end of this week.'

Excited shrieks echoed throughout the dressing-room, and Danielle returned to congratulate them after she had appeared on the platform to receive her share of the applause, but Alexa could not participate in this joyous moment. Her anxiety had intensified, and it had lodged like a weight in her chest.

Revil Bradstone's cold, contemptuous eyes had haunted her relentlessly for three long years. She had never forgotten, and she never would forget that night when she had fled from James Henderson's hotel bedroom to collide with Revil Bradstone in the dimly lit passage. It was a terrifying nightmare which often awakened her in the middle of the night when she would find that her body was drenched with perspiration. Always, those nightmares were followed by the memory of the icy condemnation and contempt in Revil Bradstone's eyes.

'Are you not happy for me, Alexa?' Madame Véronique's quietly spoken query made Alexa realise that she was almost the only one left in the dressing-room of Salon Danielle.

She had changed into the silky magenta jumpsuit in which she had arrived at the salon earlier that afternoon, but she had almost no recollection of doing so. 'I am very happy for you, Madame,' she assured her mentor, 'and you know that I shall live through every anxious moment with you until you are informed of Bradstone's decision.'

'Then why, may I ask, is there so much sadness in your lovely eyes, *chérie*?'

'Perhaps the excitement and the tension has made me remember incidents in the past that are best forgotten, Madame,' Alexa confessed in her soft, clear voice, and this was partially the truth, but not entirely.

Madame Véronique was fully aware of the unfortunate incident in Alexa's past, but Alexa had never told her about Revil Bradstone. The look in his eyes that night in the dimly lit passage had cut too deep to speak about it to anyone.

'What is past is past. We can never go back to alter the situation which had led us to make the decision we regret so much now, and we must learn not only to live with our mistakes, but to learn from them as well. You were nineteen then, and a mere child,' Madame reminded Alexa with a warm, affectionate smile. 'You are twenty-two now, and you are, I am sure, a little wiser. You will not make the same mistake twice, and that is how it should be. So go home, *chérie*, take a relaxing bath, and rest this evening. We have plenty of work to do tomorrow, and there must be no dark shadows in or around the eyes. And *that* is an *order*!'

'Yes, Madame.'

Alexa had forced herself to smile, but her smile was gone a few minutes later when she stepped into the busy Johannesburg street, and drew her coat about her to ward off the winter chill in the air. It was the thought of the heavy traffic at that time of the afternoon that had made her decide to take a bus rather than drive herself in her small Opel to Salon Danielle earlier that day, but she was not thinking about the traffic as she walked towards the bus stop. Her mind was whirling in mad, anxious circles, awakening memories, and stabbing at wounds which had never healed.

Her one-bedroomed flat in Hillbrow was comfortably but not expensively furnished. The pale pink of the padded sofa and armchairs blended well with the rich cream of the shaggy carpet and the draped curtains. In the small bedroom the padded headboard of her single bed was of the same pale pink. Pink was Alexa's favourite colour. It was a soothing, restful shade, but it was incapable of soothing her on that particular evening. She had soaked in a hot bath and, dressed in her nightgown and a warm, quilted robe, she made a sandwich with left-over chicken, and poured herself a glass of milk. She watched a programme on TV while she ate her sandwich and drank her milk, but she eventually switched off the set and sagged down into her chair with her long shapely legs stretched out in front of her. Her mind was persistent in dredging up the past and, sighing, she let it have its way.

Alexa had been nineteen, as Madame Véronique had pointed out that afternoon. Her parents had died when she was in her early teens, and the seaside hotel owned by a distant uncle and aunt had become her home during the holidays away from boarding school. She had been reasonably happy, helping out where she could, or simply lazing on the beach when she was not needed.

That was how she had intended to spend the Christmas holidays after she had taken her final exams. She had not yet decided what she wanted to do with her life, and her uncle and aunt had been quite happy for her to stay on at their hotel until she had made a decision about her future.

She would never forget that fateful holiday. It was branded in her mind as if with fire. She had been so incredibly innocent and trusting, and her warm, naturally friendly disposition had made her a favourite amongst the holiday guests. Madame Véronique had been one of the hotel guests during those steamy weeks in December prior to Christmas, and so had James Henderson. He had been a man of thirty-five, suave, well-spoken, and obviously wealthy, but he had been visibly unhappy. He had needed no prompting to spill his tale of woe one afternoon when Alexa had served him his tea in the shady garden of the hotel, and she had listened sympathetically and with the compassion of someone who had known suffering. His wife had lost the child she had been carrying, and from that moment onwards their marriage had taken a severe downward plunge. He had done everything possible to save their shaky marriage, and this separation had been arranged in the hope that it might bring his wife to her senses.

Alexa had felt sorry for him and, innocent and inexperienced as she had been, she had spent more time with him than with any of the other guests. For Alexa it had been purely platonic, an act of kindness and consideration which she would have displayed to any one of the other guests had their circumstances been similar, and no one, least of all her uncle and aunt, had thought to warn her that she might be involving herself in something which she was too youthful and too inexperienced to cope with.

One hot, sultry evening, when Alexa had served James Henderson his after dinner coffee out on the darkened terrace, he had groaned and doubled up with what had appeared to be excruciating stomach cramps. Frightened and deeply concerned, Alexa had not hesitated when he had asked her to help him up to his room. With her slender body taking the brunt of his weight, she had practically dragged him up the stairs to his room.

'I'll get reception to call a doctor,' she had said anxiously when she had at last lowered him on to his bed.

'I don't need a doctor, you little idiot,' he had laughed almost satanically, leaping to his feet and slamming the door shut. 'It's *you* I need.'

What had followed was a nightmare she would never forget. Too shocked to utter a sound, Alexa had fought against his superior male strength, and she had been sickened to her very soul by the wet, passionate kisses she had been incapable of avoiding. He had pulled her down on to the bed, but she had miraculously succeeded in escaping from him. James Henderson, breathing heavily and his lips drawn back in an ugly snarl, had leapt to his feet to lunge at her again. His hands had clutched at the front of her blouse, ripping off the buttons so that they scattered across the floor while she struck out at him in abject terror, and it was at this precise moment that his estranged wife walked into the room. Wilma Henderson had, for some obscure reason, ignored the look of terror on Alexa's white face. She had also ignored the obvious fact that Alexa had been trying to escape from James, and her accusation echoed in Alexa's mind as if it had been voiced yesterday instead of three years ago.

'You little slut!' Wilma Henderson had hissed furiously. 'You have not heard the last of me, and *you*, James, will pay dearly for your infidelity!'

Alexa had fled from the room with a mixture of terror and relief, but, in the passage, she had collided with the tall, solid frame of Revil Bradstone. Her frightened glance had registered his extraordinary good looks when his hands had steadied her, but his eyes had burned down into hers with such contempt that she had known she would remember it for the rest of her life.

Her uncle and aunt had not believed her innocent of the charges laid against her and, since no one had witnessed the incident on the terrace which had led to Alexa's presence in James Henderson's bedroom, Alexa had been condemned almost without a hearing. She was instructed to leave the premises, and it was at that point that Madame Véronique had stepped in like a guardian angel to take charge of the situation. Madame had been the only one to believe in Alexa's innocence, and Alexa had confided in her, omitting only the incident in the passage involving Revil Bradstone. She could not talk about that, it had cut too deep into her young soul.

'Have you ever considered modelling as a career?' Madame had asked. 'I have been watching you closely for some time. You are of the right height and proportions, and you move with a natural grace that some take years to acquire. If you come with me to my agency in Johannesburg I will teach you all you need to know to become a successful mannequin.'

Alexa had accepted Madame Véronique's offer like a drowning person clutching at any available straw for safety, and she had never regretted her decision . . . until now!

She sighed and got up to take her empty glass and her plate into the kitchen to wash them, but her mind continued its relentless grind through the past. James Henderson had committed suicide less than a month after that incident in the hotel. It had been in all the newspapers, with numerous photographs accompanying the lengthy, detailed article, and this was how Alexa had discovered the identity of the man with the cold, contemptuous eyes. Wilma Henderson was a member of the wealthy and influential Bradstone family, and Revil Bradstone, Chairman of Bradstone Promotions, was her brother.

Madame Véronique had never made a secret of the fact that a modelling contract with Bradstone Promotions was what she was aiming at. To acquire it would necessitate a second meeting between Alexa and Revil Bradstone, and Alexa had feared it from the start, not for her own sake, but for Madame Véronique's.

Alexa sighed again as she left the small kitchen and went to her bedroom. She sat down wearily in front of the dressing-table and gently massaged a little night-cream into her forehead, her cheeks, and her throat. Her nose was small and straight, and her chin was firm but nicely rounded. Her eyes were, however, her most arresting feature. They could at times be mysterious and provocative while still projecting that core of innocence, but it would take a discerning eye to notice the deep shadows and the pain that often lurked in their violet-blue depths.

It was once again not her appearance that occupied Alexa's thoughts at that moment. She was thinking about Revil Bradstone, and she was wondering if he would allow his decision to be influenced by his contempt for the girl who he believed had had an affair with his sister's husband.

The expected call from Bradstone Promotions did not come through the Friday morning, and Alexa, working her way methodically through a series of strenuous exercises with the rest of the girls at Madame

Véronique's studio/agency, felt the growing tension seep into her limbs until fluidity in her movements became impossible to achieve. Madame had closeted herself in her small, cluttered office when it became apparent that she had failed in her bid for the Bradstone contract, and the routine exercises came to a slow, listless halt. A low, anxious murmur erupted amongst the group of models, adding to the incredibly tense atmosphere, and Alexa felt a coldness filtering into her body long before Lucille Upton glanced at her.

'You are closer to Madame Véronique than any of us. Why don't you talk to her and find out if there's anything we can do?'

Alexa swallowed nervously, and nodded.

The door to Madame Véronique's office stood slightly ajar, and Alexa wiped her damp palms against the sides of her black tights before she tapped lightly on the door and entered.

Madame Véronique was standing at the window, staring down at the traffic in the street below with her back turned to Alexa, and her ringed hands were gripping the windowsill so tightly her knuckles were white.

'Madame?' Alexa made her presence known to the woman who had obviously been so deep in thought that she had not heard the knock on the door, and Madame Véronique turned slowly to face Alexa.

Madame's features revealed her age at that moment. She looked old and weary, and her brave, twisted little smile brought a lump to Alexa's throat.

'We did not get the contract.' Madame explained the reason for her despairing attitude, and Alexa paled.

'You don't know that for sure, Madame.'

'I am convinced this is so. I was told we would know

their decision before noon today, and it is now twelve-thirty.'

It's my fault! Alexa told herself fiercely. If Madame's suspicions are correct, then it's because of me that she didn't get the contract she desired so much!

'I'm sorry, Madame,' she said bitterly and, turning slowly, she walked back to where the other girls were waiting anxiously to hear her news.

Their reactions ranged from furious indignation to tears of disappointment, but Alexa did not linger to impart her own feelings on the matter. She showered and dressed, and left the studio without saying anything to anyone to drive directly to her flat.

Alexa could be accused of being timid and shy, but no one could ever accuse her of being a coward. If *she* was the cause of Bradstone Promotions' indecision, then it was up to *her* to do something about it, even if it meant that she had to confront the one man in the world she had hoped never to meet again.

She looked up the telephone number of Bradstone Promotions in the directory and, lifting the receiver to her ear, she punched it out quickly.

'I'd like to speak to Mr Bradstone, please,' she told the switchboard operator seconds later.

'I'll put you through to Mr Bradstone's secretary.'

The line went dead, and moments later a lilting female voice said, 'Mr Bradstone's office, good morning.'

'I'd like to make an appointment to see Mr Bradstone,' Alexa informed his secretary.

'In connection with what is this?'

'It's private and rather urgent.'

'Your name, please?'

'Alexa Drew.'

'Would you wait a moment, please?'

The line went dead with a click, and Alexa bit down

hard on her quivering lip with small, perfect white teeth. She was quaking inwardly with nerves, but it was too late to change her mind.

'Hello, Miss Drew? Are you there?'

'I'm here.' *Just*, Alexa could have added cynically.

'Mr Bradstone is free at four-thirty this afternoon,' the lilting female voice informed Alexa. 'Would that time be suitable for you?'

'It will be perfect, thank you.'

Alexa replaced the receiver with a shaky hand. She had done it! She was going to see Revil Bradstone that afternoon, and she could only pray that the outcome of this meeting would be favourable for Madame Véronique.

She dressed with care that afternoon for her confrontation with Revil Bradstone. She wore a fashionable, baggy linen jacket in pale salmon with a matching flared skirt, and a coffee-coloured lace camisole. Tiny pearl studs gleamed in her shell-like ears, and she had pinned a pearl brooch to the lapel of the jacket. As always, when she was not modelling, she used her make-up sparingly, and she chose a lipstick which was a shade darker than the colour of her outfit.

Alexa was nervous, and there was no sense in denying it to herself. She glanced up at the tall, impressive building which housed the offices and various departments of Bradstone Promotions, and she entered it with a great deal of trepidation. Potted palms and tinkling fountains welcomed her, but they did not ease the tension inside her when she asked directions to Revil Bradstone's office and was told to take the lift up to the twenty-second floor. She stepped into the steel cage and pressed the required button. The doors slid shut silently, imprisoning her, and she had a sickening feeling that her stomach had been left behind on the ground floor when the lift swept her upwards towards her destination.

Revil Bradstone's secretary was seated in a spacious and decorative foyer. Screens partitioned off her desk from the rest of the area, and she smiled prettily when Alexa approached her.

'My name is Alexa Drew, and I have an appointment with Mr Bradstone at four-thirty.'

'Oh, yes.' Her glance took in the cool elegance of Alexa's appearance with a certain amount of envy. 'You're a little early, and Mr Bradstone has someone with him at the moment, but he should be free any minute now if you don't mind waiting.'

Alexa nodded and lowered herself into a leather armchair against the opposite wall. She picked up the latest *Time* magazine and opened it with an air of deceptive casualness, but she was too nervous to do more than make a pretence of reading.

She did not have long to wait. A lean young man with untidy brown hair stormed out of the office and closed the door behind him with an angry, decisive movement.

'I'm lucky I still have my head on my shoulders,' he scowled in passing at the pretty girl behind the desk. 'The boss is in one of his foul moods this afternoon.'

That did not sound very promising, and Alexa's nervousness escalated to a height of anxiety. If Revil Bradstone was in one of his foul moods, then she had very little hope of succeeding in her quest, and the thought of failure before she had actually made the attempt was unpalatable.

Revil Bradstone's pretty, dark-haired secretary stopped typing to lift the telephone receiver on her desk, and she pressed one of the numerous buttons. 'Miss Drew is waiting to see you, Mr Bradstone.' She replaced the receiver a second later and smiled across at Alexa. 'You may go in.'

'Thank you,' Alexa murmured as she rose slowly to her feet and walked towards the panelled door, but she was not quite sure what she had thanked the girl for. She felt as if she were walking, unarmed, into a lion's den, and she wondered if Daniel, just for one fleeting second, had lost his faith in God to encounter this suffocating fear which was making her heart pound wildly against her ribs.

I'm doing this for Madame Véronique, she had to remind herself sternly and, opening the panelled door, she walked into the office with its modern steel and leather furniture.

The walls were a pale grey, the carpet a deep complementary blue, but her attractive surroundings seemed to fade away into a mist when she halted abruptly at the sight of the man who stood staring out of the window with his back turned resolutely towards her.

'Don't hover!' he barked, his voice deep, well-modulated, and bitingly cold. 'Come in and close the door!'

Alexa did as she was told, her hand shaking visibly, and her teeth clenched so tightly together that her jaw ached when she took a few paces across the carpeted floor. She stared in something between appreciation and awe at the wide-shouldered, lean-hipped man in the white shirt with the sleeves rolled up to his elbows. His hair was so dark it was almost black, and it grew strongly into his neck to touch the collar of his expensive shirt. Short dark hair curled against the tanned skin of his forearms and against the back of his broad, nicely shaped hands, and the gold watch strapped to his strong, sinewy wrist caught the afternoon sun and reflected it against the wall beside him.

Revil Bradstone turned at that moment and stepped away from the window so that she could see his cold eyes raking her in a most uncomplimentary manner from her ash-blonde hair piled stylishly on her head, down to the shoes that matched the colour of her outfit. He was deliberately making her feel cheap, as if she were something that belonged solely on a street corner, and the desire to turn and run had never been stronger, but she forced herself to remain where she was.

Her cool, direct gaze didn't falter even though her insides were shaking uncontrollably. Revil Bradstone was a devastatingly attractive man of about thirty-five, and his features were strongly and perfectly moulded. His high-bridged nose was straight, the jaw square and resolute, and there was a hint of cruelty in the thin-lipped mouth despite the sensuous curl to his lower lip. It was commonly known that he preferred long, intimate relationships with women rather than tying himself down to the permanent bondage of marriage, and Alexa wondered at the reason for his aversion.

'It amazes me that you had the nerve to request this meeting,' he remarked contemptuously, seating himself in the leather swivel chair behind his desk and gesturing her into a chair in a way that convinced her he would have preferred to tell her to get out of his office.

Alexa seated herself in the leather armchair, relieved to take her weight off her shaky legs, and she clasped her handbag tightly in her lap to control the tremor in her hands. 'I think you know why I'm here, Mr Bradstone.'

'Do I?' he smiled derisively, tugging at the knot in his sober silver-grey tie and undoing the collar button of his shirt. 'I'm a very busy man, Miss Drew. A thousand projects have to pass through my hands daily, and you expect me to develop psychic powers where you're concerned?'

'I work for Madame Véronique.'

'Do you?'

Alexa's hands tightened on her handbag. Revil Bradstone's pretended ignorance was beginning to annoy her, but she had to stay calm if she wanted to accomplish what she had set out to do.

'Madame Véronique should have been informed this morning of your decision with regard to the contract for the André Dacre spring collection. The delay has convinced her that your decision has been unfavourable to her agency, and if this is so, then I want to know if I am the cause of it. Am I?' Alexa's insides were knotted with tension and anxiety, but her features were composed, and her faintly husky voice was deceptively calm. 'Have you decided against using Madame Véronique's modelling agency because you discovered that I happen to work for her?'

The smile that curved his sensuous mouth made her realise that the pretence was over. The swords of battle were being drawn, but it was, however, going to be a very unfair battle. Revil Bradstone would be on the attack with all the power stacked on his side, and Alexa had to resign herself to the knowledge that she would be on the defensive, and pleading, in a humiliating way, for mercy.

CHAPTER TWO

ALEXA faced her adversary across the wide expanse of his steel desk with its padded top, and stepped into the arena once again to do battle. 'Have you given the contract to another agency?'

'That's none of your business!' Revil Bradstone answered bitingly, his smoke-grey eyes narrowed to angry slits, and Alexa felt as if she were sitting on a keg of dynamite which was threatening to explode.

'Please, Mr Bradstone, won't you reconsider your decision?' she pleaded softly and circumspectly. 'Madame Véronique is a fine, deserving woman, and it—it isn't fair that she should be punished in this way for—for something which happened in the past that had nothing whatsoever to—to do with her. I'm not here to plead my own cause, Mr Bradstone, but Madame Véronique's. I'm here also without her knowledge and her consent, but I'll do *anything* not to stand in the way of Madame getting that contract.'

'*Anything*, Miss Drew?' he asked, raising a dark, cynical eyebrow as he got up and walked round his cluttered desk to seat himself on the corner of it with his arms folded across his powerful chest.

Alexa realised too late what interpretation could be placed on her desperately worded plea, and her pale cheeks went pink with embarrassment as she haltingly tried to clarify her rash statement. 'Anything with—within the bounds of decency, yes.'

'You're a fine one to talk of decency, Alexa Drew,' Revil Bradstone announced scathingly, the icy contempt in his eyes cutting her to the quick and making her tremble inwardly. 'You're rotten to the core beneath this lovely outer shell you present to the world, and it would give me the greatest pleasure to expose you. There's a name for women like you, and I can't think of anyone it suits better. You're a——'

'*No*!' Alexa had stopped him with a strangled cry, her eyes dark pools in her ashen face. 'Don't say it! Please, I—it isn't true and, if you would let me explain, I'm sure you would realise that what you saw that night was not what you imagined.'

His cruel mouth thinned and curved in a contemptuous smile when he unfolded his arms and leaned towards her threateningly with a strong, sun-browned hand resting on the edge of the desk. 'Are you denying that I saw you running out of my brother-in-law's room that night?'

She shook her head helplessly. 'No, but——'

'Then, I presume, you want to imply that my sister is a liar, and that she didn't find you in a partially undressed state in her husband's hotel bedroom?'

Alexa remembered only too well how she must have looked that night. The buttons had been ripped savagely off her blouse during James Henderson's attempt to assault her sexually, and she had simply clutched the ends together to cover her nakedness when she had been given the opportunity to escape.

'If you would let me explain, I——'

'I don't think I care to hear your explanation,' he cut in with a savagery in his voice. 'Nothing could explain away the fact that my sister's husband committed suicide shortly after that incident, and nothing you may do or say now can ever take away the anguish my sister has suffered.'

Alexa felt every last drop of blood drain away from

her face. She had never dreamed that she would stand accused of something little short of murder, and it left her feeling utterly shattered and numb. She had no defence against this appalling accusation, and she knew that no ordinary explanation would suffice. This man would want proof. He would demand decisive evidence before he would accept the fact that she was innocent, and she could not give him what he wanted.

'About Madame Véronique.' She broke the tense silence when she had succeeded in pulling herself together to some extent. 'What do you intend to do?'

Revil Bradstone got to his feet and thrust his hands deep into his pockets when he walked away from her to stand in front of the window with his broad back facing her once again, and she stared at him with a silent prayer on her lips.

'I am not in the habit of allowing my personal feelings to become involved when a business decision has to be made, and I suspect that at this very moment Madame Véronique is being informed of our decision. The contract is hers,' he said, turning to pin Alexa to her chair with cold, narrowed eyes, and filling her with dread rather than relief. 'You said you would do *anything* if I gave the contract to Madame Véronique, and I intend to hold you to that promise despite the fact that you in no way influenced our decision.'

Alexa stared at him warily, mentally circling his threatening statement, and what it might be implying. 'I—I don't think I quite understand what you hope to gain by holding me to that—that promise.'

'You came here this afternoon and attempted to sell yourself to me for a contract, didn't you?' he demanded harshly.

'I—no, I——'

'Oh, yes, you did, Alexa,' he interrupted, walking

round the desk towards her, and smiling derisively down into her startled eyes. 'Your exact words were that you would do *anything* not to stand in Madame Véronique's way of getting the contract, and I'm going to hold you to that for personal reasons. You have placed yourself very nicely in my hands, and that's exactly where I have wanted you for the past three years. I'm going to make it my business to see that you suffer the agonies my sister suffered, and don't forget that I'm in a position to ruin you professionally if I should choose to do so.'

A suffocating blanket of darkness threatened to engulf her, but she fought it off valiantly. Never had anyone looked at her with such undisguised hatred, and never had she been so utterly helpless to do anything about it. Fear made the adrenalin pump faster through her veins, and it activated her mind as nothing else had ever done. There was only one way he could make her suffer; only one way he could ruin her life and her career completely, and she could not bear to think about it.

'Mr Bradstone, I——'

'Revil,' he corrected, his mouth twisting savagely as if he had read her mind. 'You might as well start calling me Revil since we're going to spend a great deal of time with each other during the next few months.'

'You are making a grave mistake, and you'll regret it,' she protested, her voice a mere breath of a whisper, but he had heard her.

'No, Alexa,' he contradicted in that bitingly cold voice as he seated himself on the corner of the desk close to her. '*You* made a grave mistake when you had that affair with my brother-in-law, and *you* are going to regret it for the rest of your life.'

'I never had an——'

'Spare me the lies, and get out!'

Alexa shrank inwardly from the icy contempt in his

eyes, and she rose slowly to her feet. Revil Bradstone stood up at the same time, and Alexa, five feet six inches in her stockinged feet, found that she had to tilt her head back some distance to look up into the good-looking, but harsh features of the man who had stated quite bluntly that he intended to ruin her. If it had been anyone else, then she might have been tempted to believe that it was nothing but an idle threat, but Alexa knew instinctively that Revil Bradstone was not a man to make threats and not carry them out to the last detail.

Fear clutched at her insides and, turning from him, she walked out of his office without saying a word. She could not have spoken even if she had wanted to. Her throat had seized up, and she could do no more than nod and force a smile to her stiff lips when she passed Revil Bradstone's secretary on her way to the lift.

Alexa drove herself back to her flat, but she wondered afterwards how she had managed to do so without having an accident. Her mind had not been on her driving. She had been thinking about the terrible things Revil Bradstone had said, and she was afraid.

The first thing she did when she got to her flat was to take a shower. She soaped herself, feeling as if she had been soiled by his accusations, but the jet of water pummelling her taut body did not quite reach her soul. She had been branded a . . .! Her mind refused to conjure up those defiling words, any one of which Revil Bradstone might have used if she had not stopped him, and she groaned as she stepped under the jet of warm water to let it spill from her head and down along her too-slender body with the small, high breasts and narrow waist. She had no reason to feel ashamed, but she felt as if she was drowning in shame at that moment.

Two hours later she was sitting huddled on a chair in the darkened lounge of her ninth-floor flat. Her long legs

were curled in under her, and the muted sound of the
Hillbrow traffic mingled with her thoughts. She hadn't
made herself anything to eat; the thought of food had
nauseated her, and she had made coffee instead, but the
cup stood untouched on the small table beside her.

Alexa jumped nervously when the telephone started
ringing, and she glanced at the digital clock on her hi-fi
set as she reached out to switch on the reading lamp
beside her. It was eight-thirty. Every nerve in her body
felt as if it had suddenly become centred at the pit of her
stomach, and she let the telephone ring for several
agonising seconds before she scraped together sufficient
courage to answer it.

'Alexa, *chérie*, I had almost given up hope of finding
you at home,' Madame Véronique exclaimed, her
accent more pronounced in her excitement, and Alexa
sagged against the wall to steady herself as Madame
continued speaking. 'I have had the most extraordinary,
and the most wonderful news for you. I received a call
from Bradstone Promotions, and I have been trying to
contact you since four-thirty this afternoon. There was a
delay in making the decision, but we do have the
contract after all. Is that not wonderful, *chérie*?'

'Wonderful,' Alexa agreed, realising what a fool she
had been to think it was necessary for her to intercede on
Madame's behalf, and quaking inwardly with apprehension about her own future. 'I'm so happy for you,
Madame.'

Revil Bradstone had not deceived her, that was
something which counted in his favour, and she had only
herself to blame for walking into a trap which he had not
deliberately set for her, but the trap had been there all
the same, waiting and ready to be sprung at the given
moment.

'Are you not also happy for yourself, Alexa, and for

the rest of my girls who have worked so very hard?'

'Naturally, Madame.'

'Sometimes I think I would like to shake you, Alexa!' Madame Véronique announced in an exasperated voice. 'You are always so calm and controlled. Never, since that unfortunate incident, do you show when you are happy, or when you are sad. There is no spontaneity, and your beautiful, warm heart has been stored away in ice. Why did you do this to yourself, *chérie?*'

Alexa withdrew deeper into her self-created shell. 'It is safer that way, Madame.'

'Safer?' Madame Véronique demanded indignantly. 'Safer for whom, may I know?'

'For me, Madame,' Alexa answered simply.

'*Mon Dieu!*' Madame exploded in Alexa's ear. 'You have to *live* your life, Alexa. It is there for you to *enjoy!* You smile when it is expected of you, but you never laugh. Why do you not laugh any more, *chérie?*'

'Perhaps there has been nothing to laugh about, Madame,' Alexa explained, an unexpected lump settling uncomfortably in her throat.

'And you are always so polite, and so *calm!*' Madame accused exasperatedly. '*Dieu*, Alexa, do not go to sleep on life, or you might regret it.'

Long after their conversation had ended, Alexa was still standing beside the telephone table thinking about what her mentor had said. It was not true, she was not always calm and composed. Inwardly she was still the same compassionate, impulsive girl Madame Véronique had taken under her protective wing, but outwardly she had learned to control her emotions. It was her impulsive, warm-hearted nature which had led her into trouble three years ago, and she had vowed that it would not happen again.

It was for her own safety that she had adopted a

retiring attitude, but it was her strong sense of justice that had led her to make that appointment to see Revil Bradstone, and that, too, had now involved her in something which made her shudder and trembled inwardly with fear. It seemed as if the nightmare was never going to end; Revil Bradstone was going to make sure of that, and for Alexa there would be no relief in tomorrow.

A scream woke Alexa in the night, and she shot up in bed, her quivering body drenched in perspiration. It took only a moment to realise that it had been her own scream she had heard. She had not had such a vivid, frightening dream in weeks, and she sagged back weakly against the pillows as the memory of it spilled through her mind. She was in court, testifying to her innocence on a charge of murder, and Revil Bradstone was the judge and the jury. His eyes were cold and contemptuous, and throughout her plea of innocence his harsh voice rang out in the court-room. 'Liar! Liar! Liar!' he had shouted in her terrifying dream. 'The verdict is *guilty*, and I sentence you, Alexa Drew, to a life of suffering from which there will be no escape!'

It was a cold June night, but it was not the coldness of that wintry night which was making Alexa shiver uncontrollably. She put on her quilted gown, and the bitter taste of gall was in her mouth when she got out of bed, pushed her feet into soft mules, and went to the kitchen. She flicked the switch against the wall, blinking and narrowing her eyes until they adjusted to the light, and she poured herself a glass of milk before she subsided on to the stool beside the counter to drink it.

What was she going to do?

Madame Véronique signed the contract with Bradstone Promotions a few days later, and work began in earnest with André Dacre. He was a sparsely built man in his early forties who was balding swiftly. He was disappointingly insignificant in appearance, but there was no doubt that he was a brilliant designer, and highly respected in his profession.

The materials André Dacre had selected for his fantastic range of garments varied from expensive cotton to the finest silk, and the colours were either bright and youthful or calm pastels. They had less than a month to prepare themselves for what was termed 'The Fashion Show of the Year', and the venue would be a banquet hall in Johannesburg's Carlton Centre.

It was an exciting as well as an exhausting project, with Madame Véronique and André Dacre shouting instructions at the eight models, and arguing between themselves, at times, about how the models were to present the garments.

André Dacre, a Capetonian, had set up shop with his two assistants in the Bradstone building for the duration of his stay in Johannesburg, and in this way Revil Bradstone could keep a critical eye on the preparations for the fashion show his company was promoting. Alexa found Revil's presence disconcerting at the rehearsals and fitting-sessions, but not once did she falter.

Madame Véronique's girls, all except Alexa, were in a constant swoon about Revil Bradstone's good looks, and quite a few of them tried a provocative approach to capture his attention, but without success.

'He's an absolute dream,' one of the girls sighed in the dressing-room late one afternoon when they were changing to go home. 'I'd give my false eyelashes to go out on a date with him.'

'Keep your false eyelashes for someone else, Pamela,' Lucille Upton warned with a knowing, faintly mocking laugh as she peeled off her tights and exchanged them for sheer pantihose. 'He hasn't been attending the rehearsals so regularly to look at you. It's our cool and beautiful Alexa he's got his eye on, if you ask me.'

Alexa's insides jolted when she sat down in front of the mirror to apply her make-up, but somehow she managed to remain outwardly calm and unperturbed by the trend of their conversation. 'You have a vivid imagination, Lucille,' she said reprovingly.

'What's the bet he asks you out on a date within the next few days?' Lucille challenged, her green eyes sparkling with amusement, but Alexa found nothing amusing at the thought of going out on a date with Revil Bradstone. It filled her instead with dread, but this was not something she was going to tell Lucille.

'Why would he do that?' Alexa asked innocently.

'Why wouldn't he?' Lucille bounced back while she brushed her auburn hair vigorously. 'I happen to know that his relationship with Carol Ross, the film and stage personality, came to a rather abrupt end some months ago, leaving him free to seek new pastures, and Revil Bradstone has a reputation for seldom being without a woman in his arms and in his bed. Oh, I know you're not his type, and that you're still a virgin in mind and body,' Lucille added hastily when Alexa tried to interrupt her, 'but I believe he can be very persuasive.'

A virgin in mind and body! There had been nothing sarcastic in Lucille's choice of words, but Alexa had cringed inwardly. She *was* still a virgin, it was something the rest of the girls had often teased her about, but Revil Bradstone believed the opposite, and Alexa could almost hear his derisive laughter had he heard Lucille's remark.

'It's in bad taste to discuss a man like Revil Bradstone behind his back, and to speculate like that about his personal life,' Alexa scolded Lucille gently while she applied a light touch of lipstick to her generous mouth.

'And neither should you believe everything you read in the newspapers.'

'Good heavens, Alexa! One might be inclined to think you cared for the man the way you leap to his defence,' Lucille teased, and Alexa paled visibly as she replaced the cap on her lipstick and dropped it into her bag.

Aware that they had an inquisitive audience of six, Alexa chose her words carefully. 'I care about people, and I believe in privacy. I also know that many unjust and untrue statements have found their way into the press, and for this reason I don't care to judge people from what I've read about them in the newspapers.'

Was she defending Revil Bradstone? Or was she defending herself in advance for whatever the future might have in store for her? Alexa wondered about this as she said goodnight and left.

Lucille's prediction came true much sooner than Alexa had expected. Her doorbell rang at a quarter to seven that evening and when she opened the door as far as the safety chain would allow she found Revil Bradstone standing on her doorstep.

Her heart was racing and her hands were shaking as she slipped back the chain to let him in, and fear had taken a strangle-hold on her throat that prevented her from speaking as she stared up at the tall, dynamic chairman of Bradstone Promotions, who looked as if he had come to her directly from the office, since he was wearing the same expensively tailored brown suit she had noticed him wearing earlier that day.

Revil's virile masculinity appealed to most women, and the weakness in Alexa's knees was not entirely due to fear when he brushed past her to enter her flat. From their very first meeting, three years ago, she had been aware of that powerful aura of maleness about him and, if she were honest with herself, she would have to admit that her youthful, feminine body had responded with a leaping of the senses for that brief second before the contempt in his eyes had frozen her natural instincts.

She was aware that he was observing her with a strange look in his smoke-grey eyes, and she swallowed nervously. 'I'm afraid I wasn't expecting you, Mr Bradstone.'

'Revil,' he corrected, his smiling, penetrating glance raking her from head to foot as if he were assessing her body beneath her casual clothes. 'Didn't I make it clear that we would be seeing a great deal more of each other in the near future?'

'Yes, you did, and I never thought for one moment that you were a man to make idle threats,' she answered him in an admirably calm voice, but her face had paled at the memory of the accusations he had made, and her pulse was much too fast for comfort.

'Nice little place you have here. It's restful and homely.' He smiled twistedly, and his glance was critical when he looked about him. 'And pink is a very feminine colour, which happens to suit you perfectly.'

Alexa recoiled inwardly. Was he mocking her, or was he serious? she wondered confusedly. She schooled her expression, hiding her feelings behind a cool, aloof mask when he turned to look at her, and it required every ounce of will-power she possessed to withstand that searchingly intent appraisal that left her with the humiliating feeling that he had stripped her mentally to look upon her body with a view to something which made the rhythm of her pulses quicken with fear.

His dark brows drew together in a frown as if he was angered by his own thoughts, and his sensuous mouth tightened. 'Have you had dinner?'

Bewildered by his abrupt query, she stammered, 'Well, no, I—I was about to—to make something for myself when you arrived.'

'Forget it,' he announced tersely, gesturing expressively with one strong, sun-browned hand. 'I'm in the right mood for a long, relaxing meal, and I want you to accompany me.'

Alexa felt resentment building up inside her, but it was washed away by a crushing wave of helplessness. 'I take it that's not an invitation, but an order.

'It's an invitation,' he corrected, his sensuous mouth curving in a smile that did not quite reach his eyes. 'I have never yet had to order a woman to have dinner with me when I've felt the need for female company, and I don't intend to start now. You're an attractive woman, and I desire your company at my dinner-table. Are you going to refuse me?'

Was she going to refuse him? For her own safety she ought to, but she was becoming fascinated and intrigued by the complexity of this man's character. A week ago he had savagely threatened to ruin her and make her suffer the agonies he believed she had inflicted on his sister, but his manner this evening was almost the opposite.

'I shall have to change into something more suitable.' She heard herself accepting his invitation while she glanced down at the comfortable slacks and sweater she had donned minutes before Revil's unexpected arrival.

'I'll give you ten minutes,' he said, glancing at the gold watch strapped to his strong wrist, and she fled into her bedroom, closing the door firmly behind her with a fast-beating heart.

Ten minutes, Revil had said and, not wanting to shatter his present mood, she opened her cupboard doors and took out the first thing she could lay her hands on. It was a soft woollen dress the colour of rich cream with a wide, attractively embroidered collar, and long sleeves to give her sufficient warmth on that cold evening.

Alexa touched up her make-up and glanced at her wrist-watch. She had three minutes left to do something about her hair and, pulling out the combs, she brushed it and rolled it once again into a neat chignon in the nape of her neck.

She looked calm and composed, but that was not how she felt moments later beneath the appraisal of Revil Bradstone's smoke-grey eyes. He had the ability to shatter her adult composure, to make her feel like a gauche schoolgirl, and, disconcerted, she lowered her gaze to the polished leather of his expensive, hand-made shoes.

'Let's go,' he said abruptly, and Alexa was trembling so badly he would have felt it if he had touched her when they left her flat and took the slow-moving lift down to where he had parked his champagne-coloured Jaguar.

Revil made no attempt to speak in the car during the drive to the restaurant, and his brooding silence unnerved her. She risked a quick glance at his stern profile, and wondered what he was thinking. What terrible form of retribution was he planning for her? Or was that brilliant mind embroiled in something which had nothing to do with her at all?

If Alexa had imagined that he would take her to a restaurant where he wouldn't be recognised, then she was mistaken. He took her to Santini's, a place frequented by the élite and the wealthy, and a veritable paradise for the newshounds of the press. Alexa had discovered long ago that whatever Revil Bradstone did was news. He was a powerful and respected business-man, but it was nevertheless an unsettling experience to find herself caught in a barrage of flash bulbs the moment they arrived.

A stocky-looking reporter shouldered his way through to the front of the small crowd surrounding them, and he held his pen poised over his notebook. 'Who's your new lady-friend, Mr Bradstone?'

Lady-friend; pillow-friend; mistress! The association of words spilled into Alexa's frantic mind, and she shrank inwardly, embarrassment colouring her cheeks.

'The lady's name is Alexa Drew,' Revil replied smoothly, his eyes mocking her as he slid a possessive arm about her waist, and the warmth of his hand against her side made her heart beat so hard and fast against her ribs that she was afraid he might feel it against his fingers. 'Now, would you mind letting us pass?' Revil added in a clipped voice, brushing the young man aside imperiously, but they found their way barred by yet another reporter.

'Mr Bradstone, is there any truth in the rumour that Carol Ross tried to commit suicide after you split up a few months ago?' the lanky young man demanded cheekily, and Alexa felt Revil stiffen.

'Carol Ross has always been a sensible, level-headed lady, and our relationship was not of such a nature that it would justify an attempt at suicide when we parted company,' Revil replied coldly, and this time they were allowed to enter the restaurant with its deep red and marble-white décor.

Heads turned, and curious glances followed them when they were shown to a table in a pillared alcove. She knew what everyone must be thinking, and her colour deepened. It embarrassed and it distressed her, and she had no idea how to cope with this situation.

They were given the menu to study while they waited for the bottle of red wine which Revil had ordered.

'I can tell you don't like the idea of being known as the new woman in my life,' Revil announced in a faintly derisive voice, and she forced her glance to remain cool when she raised it to his.

'That's what you want everyone to think, isn't it?'

'You misunderstand my motives, Alexa,' he smiled twistedly. 'I'm not ashamed of being seen with you in public, and it amuses me that, after tonight, everyone is going to assume you're my property.'

His property! *After tonight*! Those words had an ominous ring to them that chilled her. What else did he perhaps have planned for tonight, or was she allowing her imagination to run riot?

'Tell me about Carol Ross,' Alexa dared to question him in an attempt to take her mind off the anxiety spiralling through her. 'Did she try to commit suicide?'

'Drama is Carol's life,' he explained, his eyebrows meeting in an angry frown. 'She lives it privately as well as publicly, but suicide is not her style, and our parting was as a result of a mutual decision which did not require a dramatic finale to emphasise it.'

His deep, well-modulated voice had been cold and harsh, but a warmth had entered his eyes to make her suspect that a certain amount of fondness still lingered between Revil and Carol Ross despite the fact that their affair had ended and, whatever it was that had brought their relationship to an end, it had been accomplished in a civilised, friendly manner.

They studied the menu in silence, but Alexa had difficulty in deciding what to order. She was too aware of Revil Bradstone's forceful presence, and that masculine appeal which, as a woman, she could not ignore. She wondered idly what it would feel like to be on the receiving end of one of his warm, affectionate glances, and a strange longing stirred to life inside her, but she quelled it at once, forcing herself to concentrate on the menu.

The wine-steward appeared with the vintage wine Revil had ordered and, when their glasses were filled, she took a much needed sip to steady herself.

'Have you decided on anything, or shall I order for you?' Revil asked, and Alexa closed the menu with an inward sigh of relief.

'I'll leave the choice to you.'

Revil ordered shelled mussels in champagne sauce to start off with, and Alexa was grateful that she had an adventurous palate. As a main course they had lamb with lychees and mandarins, and it was served with a mint sauce and fresh vegetables.

Alexa could not decide whether it was the wine or the good food, but the tension seemed to ease slowly out of her body, and she was surprised to discover that, despite her nervousness, she was actually enjoying Revil's company. He questioned her about her work while they ate, and she listened while he told her about his plans for the fashion show. He was a perfect companion, and Alexa could almost have forgotten that he despised her if it had not been for that look of icy contempt which had leapt into his smoke-grey eyes when she had mentioned Madame Véronique's generous offer that ill-fated Christmas holiday three years ago.

They were drinking their coffee when she became aware of Revil staring at her over the rim of his cup with coldly assessing eyes, and she felt her nerves knotting at the pit of her stomach.

'Why are you looking at me like that?' she asked, her voice remarkably calm when she put down her cup and clenched her hands in her lap.

'You puzzle me, Alexa.'

'In what way?'

'I can understand and accept the fact that women have become as career-minded as men, and that they prefer to live with a man rather than tie themselves down to something as permanent and restricting as marriage, but the way you choose to live your life puzzles me.' He drained his cup and leaned back in his chair, his eyes as hard as steel when they trailed over her and lingered for a heart-stopping moment on her small breasts thrusting gently against the soft woollen material of her dress. 'What satisfaction do you derive from indulging in one-night stands with married men? Does the knowledge that it's forbidden provide you with some macabre excitement?'

Alexa's pale cheeks went a shade paler. 'You don't expect me to answer that, do you?'

'I do, but I also know I shan't hear the truth.' His mouth tightened into a cruel, harsh line. 'How many men have there been, Alexa?'

'There haven't been any,' she answered truthfully, but the cynical quirk of his lips told her that he did not believe her.

'Is that the image you're trying to project? The sweet little virgin, the *girl next door* everyone likes to think of as pure and untouched, while in actual fact you're a——' He broke off sharply with an exclamation of disgust that made her wince inwardly as if he had slapped her. 'God help me, but I'm going to make it my business to find out what it is that makes a girl like you what you are!'

He called for the bill, and they left immediately afterwards. Alexa sat stiff and silent beside him in his Jaguar while she fought against a strange depression. It was ten-thirty, it had been a long, exhausting day, and all she wanted at that moment was to crawl into bed to sleep and, hopefully, forget.

CHAPTER THREE

FLASHING neon signs beckoned invitingly above coffee bars and restaurants, and the amount of traffic in the well-lit Johannesburg streets indicated that, for many people, the night had only just begun. Teenagers gathered in groups on street corners, and a police patrol van cruised slowly down the busy street, its occupants on the alert.

'You've passed the turn-off to my flat.' Alexa spoke for the first time since they had left the restaurant, and in the confined space of Revil's Jaguar her voice sounded infinitely weary.

'I know that,' he answered her abruptly, turning left at the traffic lights, and driving in the opposite direction. 'We're going to my place.'

A suffocating fear clutched at her insides, and her heart was beating so hard in her throat that she could scarcely breathe. 'But—but I don't want to go to—to your place.'

'The night is still young, my dear.' His soft laughter ended abruptly when he glanced in the rear-view mirror. 'I think we're being followed by one of those newshounds.'

'Take me home! Please! I don't want him to think that I'm your ... that we're ...'

'Lovers,' he filled in mockingly when she choked on the word and had to swallow convulsively to ease the restriction in her throat. 'Quite frankly, Alexa, I couldn't care less if he chooses to believe we're lovers.'

'But that ... wouldn't ... be true,' she accused faintly, a numbness sweeping into her limbs when she began to suspect that it might well be true before this night was over.

'Since when has it become so important to you to be truthful?' he demanded with a scornful laugh that cut deep, but her chin lifted with a hint of unaccustomed defiance and pride.

'Since always,' she answered with that truthfulness Revil believed her incapable of, and a disparaging sound passed his lips.

'How well you have mastered the art of lying with that ring of sincerity in your voice,' he accused bitingly, and she turned her head to face the other way when helpless tears glistened in her eyes.

He was determined to hurt her; determined to disbelieve her, but she was not going to give him the satisfaction of seeing her crack under the pressure he exerted. She blinked away her tears and somehow succeeded in regaining a degree of outward composure, but inwardly she was fighting a losing battle against a growing apprehension and fear.

Alexa was shivering when she got out of Revil's Jaguar in the basement of a tall, grey building, and her legs were shaking beneath her when she accompanied him into the lift that would take them up to his penthouse. It was a chilly night, but it was nerves rather than the cold that had taken her in its vice-like grip. Revil leaned casually against the side of the ascending lift, his hands thrust into his pockets, and his eyes narrowed as he studied her intently. She could feel that he was silently willing her to look at him, but she held her face averted to stare fixedly at the numbers flashing above the doors. Eighteen ... nineteen ... oh, God, where was this night going to end?

The lift came to a gentle halt. The doors slid open, and Revil ushered her across a carpeted, well-lit foyer towards a heavy, panelled door. He unlocked it, and stood aside for her to precede him into his penthouse.

Alexa felt like an animal walking with complete awareness into a trap, and her nerves jarred violently when she heard him close the door behind them. The trap had been sprung, she thought crazily, and she stood staring blindly ahead of her, too nervous for the moment to take in her exquisitely furnished surroundings.

'Would you like a drink? Something to relax you?' Revil suggested, his fingers hard beneath her elbow when he led her down the three steps into the sunken lounge, and she felt a humiliating warmth sliding into her cheeks at the knowledge that he was very much aware of how she was feeling at that moment.

'No, thank you,' she declined hastily. She had had enough to drink during dinner, and she needed a clear head to cope with this frightening situation.

Revil shrugged carelessly and walked away from her towards the built-in wall units containing his television set, hi-fi and drinks cabinet, and he poured himself a whisky on ice which he swallowed down almost in one gulp.

There was nothing elaborate about the furnishings in Revil Bradstone's penthouse. The comfortably padded armchairs and sofas were covered in a dark grey, expensive-looking cloth, and chrome tables with glass tops were strategically placed on the white shaggy-haired carpet to add a simple, modern touch. The curtains were a mixture of dark and light grey, and they were partially drawn across glass sliding doors which, Alexa presumed, led out on to the penthouse's roof garden. It was very much a man's domain, masculine in décor and uncluttered, and she had to admit that she liked his taste.

'Let your hair down.'

'*What?*'

She spun round, startled almost out of her wits to find

Revil standing less than a pace away from her, and her heart missed several beats. He had taken off his jacket, his tie had been loosened, and the top buttons of his shirt had been undone to expose the dark hair curling up from his sun-bronzed chest. He was, at that moment, exuding an aura of virile sensuality which was more potent than any alcoholic drink he could have offered her, and her senses responded to it with a wildness she had difficulty in curbing.

'Take the combs out of your hair, and let it down, Alexa,' he instructed, a strange quietness in his deep voice that set her nerves on edge.

'No!' she refused, her pulse beating out a frightened and erratic rhythm at the base of her throat as she backed away from him, but Revil had anticipated her move. Steely fingers snaked about her wrist, jerking her towards him, and the woody scent of his masculine cologne attacked her senses while his free hand reached for the combs holding her silky hair in place. 'No ... please ... don't do that!'

Her plea was ignored. His hand was in her hair, whipping out first the one comb, and then the other so that her hair tumbled down to hang in soft, silvery waves to below her shoulders. She knew that she must look as vulnerable as she felt, and her eyes, a deep violet-blue, stared up into his reproachfully.

'My God!' he breathed, his mouth twisting derisively when he released her unexpectedly. 'That air of innocence you project is even stronger when you have your hair down like this, but we both know that it's a false image, don't we, Alexa?'

Revil Bradstone seemed to bring out the worst in Alexa with his continual accusations, and a fountain of unaccustomed anger welled up inside her, forcing her to retaliate.

'You have set yourself up as judge and jury because of

one incident you happened to witness, and you've convicted me without a hearing.'

'If you want a hearing so badly, then you've got it.' He dropped her tortoise-shell combs on to the glass table, and slumped into a chair, smiling cynically as he gestured expressively with his hands. 'Let's hear *your* version of what happened that night Wilma found you in James's room.'

Alexa was suddenly a quivering mass of nerves now that she had been given the opportunity to speak in her own defence. The last time she had talked about that incident in the hotel she had had Madame Véronique as a receptive, understanding audience, but Revil's cynical expression was not in the least encouraging.

Her legs felt as if they were wobbling like jelly beneath her, and she subsided weakly on to the sofa behind her. Revil was displaying an extraordinary tolerance while he waited for her to start speaking and, summoning what little courage she had left, she began to relate the incidents which had led up to her presence that night in James Henderson's room. She started haltingly, her voice growing stronger as she went along, but she stopped in mid-sentence when she noticed the smirk on Revil's face at the mention of James Henderson's bogus stomach cramps.

'You don't believe me! You don't *want* to believe me!' she accused, leaping to her feet with her hands clenching and unclenching spasmodically at her sides, and her eyes dark with disappointment and anger in her white face. 'Did it ever occur to you that your judgment might be faulty?'

'It did,' he admitted, smiling cynically as he stretched his long legs out in front of him, 'but I spoke to James a few days before he stupidly ended his life, and I made him tell me everything. He told me how you had practically thrown yourself at him at every available opportunity, that you had made it almost impossible for him to refuse you when you went to his room that night and, by all accounts, he wasn't the only married man in the hotel you coerced into a brief and tawdry affair.'

Alexa's face was ashen, and she was shaking uncontrollably while she digested those sickening lies told by a man she had once felt sorry for. 'That's not true! I never threw myself at him in the way he said. He was——'

'Oh, come off it, Alexa!' Revil laughed harshly. 'James had his faults like everyone else, but he had always been a devoted husband. You caught him at a time when he was feeling low, and you led him on until he couldn't resist you. Why don't you admit it, instead of lying about it?'

She drew a deep, steadying breath, and injected a calmness into her voice which she was far from experiencing. 'James Henderson was a filthy liar and, if he had been alive today, I would have taken him to court on a charge of defamation of character.'

'Brave words, Alexa, but I'm afraid they don't convince me,' Revil sneered, getting up to pour himself another whisky which he did not down as swiftly as he had done the first. 'James is dead, and that makes you feel safe to make such an accusation, but had he been alive you wouldn't have had the nerve to lay such a charge against him.'

'Did your sister believe him?' she asked warily, recalling the look on Wilma Henderson's attractive features when she had walked into the hotel bedroom that night, and wondering why she had been so very determined to interpret the situation incorrectly.

'My sister was not in a fit state at the time to discuss the matter,' Revil interrupted her disturbed thoughts. 'She was in the process of trying to recover from the shock of losing the child she had been carrying when she found you in his room that night, and she went nearly out of her mind. She was adamant that she wanted a divorce, and nothing James or I could say would make her change her mind. I think that was what finally broke James, and I suspect that Wilma has never forgiven herself for being so harsh on him.' His features became distorted with a savage anger as he swallowed down the remainder of his drink and thumped the empty glass down on to the cupboard. 'I don't suppose you stopped to think that your actions that night might have such far-reaching effects. I don't suppose you have *ever* given it a thought in your determined pursuit of those stolen hours of physical pleasure.'

It was incredible that she could stand there listening to him while he exposed her character for what he considered it to be and, like a dirty piece of linen, tore it to shreds. Anger blazed in his eyes, but it was accompanied by a strangely tormented look, and compassion stirred within her. He loved his sister, and he had firmly believed everything that Wilma and James Henderson had told him. There was no doubt in his mind; there never would be, and Alexa envied Wilma Henderson for having the unfaltering loyalty of a brother like Revil Bradstone.

'I'm not like that, Revil,' she pleaded with him.

'I'm not like that, Revil,' he mimicked her voice cruelly, lessening the distance between them in a few quick strides to slide his hands about her slender throat, and to tip her face up with his thumbs beneath her chin. 'When you look at me like that with your clear, sweetly innocent eyes I could almost believe you. The crazy fact is I actually *want* to believe you, but when I think of what you did to my sister . . .' His lips curled back in a savage snarl to expose strong, white teeth. 'I could kill you!'

His fingers tightened about her throat.

'Please!' she begged him, her voice no more than a

whisper. 'You're ... hurting ... me!'

'A part of me wants to hurt you so badly you'll carry the mental and physical scars with you into your grave, but there's also a part of me that simply wants you.'

Her frightened eyes were raised to his. She was not in a position to defend herself against him when his arm whipped about her waist to jerk her up against him, and coming into contact with his hard, muscle-toned body sent shock waves coursing along her nervous system. His eyes, blazing with a strange mixture of fury and desire, burned down into hers for a brief second before he lowered his head and claimed her soft mouth in a savage, bruising kiss that made her head spin.

Alexa clutched a little wildly at his broad shoulders for support, and touching him like that, feeling the play of those taut muscles through the thin, expensive cotton of his shirt, sent an odd thrill of pleasure racing through her that overshadowed the bruising agony of his mouth crushing her lips against her teeth. The warm, clean smell of his male body stirred her senses, and her scalp tingled when his hand moved through her hair.

The pressure of his mouth against hers eased suddenly, and she felt the tip of his tongue sliding along her lips, parting them to caress the tender flesh he had bruised moments before. It was such an erotic and intimate intrusion that she trembled with the sweet and unexpected pleasure of it, and his hands slid down to her buttocks to draw her closer to his aroused body.

Alexa was confused, her emotions in a turmoil, and she was even more confused a moment later when she was thrust aside with a force that made her stagger backwards before she regained her somewhat precarious balance on unsteady legs.

'Damn you, Alexa!' His voice was harsh and grating, his eyes a little wild as they burned their way down her slender body. 'I wish to God I knew how you manage to do it!'

'How I manage to—to do what?' she asked, feeling totally bewildered.

'For a woman who has so much experience to her credit your lips are almost as innocent as a child's and, together with that look of innocence in your eyes, you're quite a potent mixture.'

But I am innocent! she wanted to shout at him, but she was not in the habit of staging an aggressive display, and she chose a quieter, slightly mocking counter-attack.

'It must be quite a blow to your vengeful, egotistical mind to discover that you can actually want the woman you profess to feel nothing but contempt for.'

Alexa was alarmed by her own remark, and her innate shyness came into play at the thought that she could have voiced the knowledge she had gained during their close embrace. Her cheeks flamed during the ensuing silence, but Revil appeared not to notice. He was staring fixedly instead at a point above her head as if he could not bear to look at her for the moment.

'I've known from that night you came careering out of James's room that you were the kind of girl I could want badly.' He broke the strained silence between them in a low, savage voice, and the eyes that met hers at last were icy with that now familiar contempt. 'For three years I've lived with that damnable knowledge, and it's been like a cancer growing inside me, but let me assure you, Alexa, I despise myself for it almost as much as I despise you.'

Alexa's legs gave way beneath her, and she sat down rather heavily on the sofa behind her with her colour coming and going in rapid succession while she stared incredulously up into the face of the man standing a few paces away from her. She was, incredibly, hovering somewhere between laughter and tears, and she fought a fierce battle with herself to surrender to neither of those desires.

Revil's sensuous mouth thinned in a smile of self-derision which was almost too painful to observe. 'Shocking, isn't it, that I could have felt such an instant attraction for someone who had just ruined two lives?'

'No, it isn't shocking, because I felt it too,' she whispered, recalling the way her youthful body had responded to Revil's nearness that night three years ago.

'Do you know something, Alexa?' His expression was grave except for a faintly sardonic gleam in his eyes when he took her hands and drew her to her feet. 'This time I believe you're telling the truth.'

If gaining Revil's confidence, and if convincing him of her innocence could be compared to climbing a ladder, then she had stepped up on to the first rung, but she had no time to linger on that thought. His hands circled her waist, their warmth activating those tremors that quickened her pulse, and there was no desire in her mind to evade the mouth that descended on hers with a sensual pressure to tease her lips apart for the erotic and intimate invasion of his tongue.

She felt light-headed as the blood flowed faster through her veins, and strange things were happening to her body when his hands slid down across her hips to her thighs and up again to draw her close against his hard frame. She had never known that a man could make her feel this way, so free of all her shyness and inhibitions, but she was not so sure that she ought to rejoice about the fact that it was Revil Bradstone who had awakened these feelings in her.

Her arms went up of their own volition, her fingers losing themselves in the dark hair at the nape of his neck. She did not pause to query what she was doing, it seemed so much easier to let her natural instincts take charge, and a little gasp of pleasure escaped her when his mouth left hers to nibble at her ear and the sensitive cord of her throat.

Revil's mouth returned to hers, drugging her, and setting her on fire as he edged her back against the sofa and lowered her on to it to hold her there with the heavy weight of his heated, aroused body. His fingers worked their way through her hair splayed like thick silver strands against the contrasting dark grey of the sofa. He stroked the pale, smooth skin of her throat, awakening tiny nerves to the pleasure of his touch, and she did not have the will to resist when his fingers explored lower until they came up against the barrier which the wide collar of her dress provided. He groaned impatiently against her mouth, and slid his hands beneath her to pull down the zip of her dress.

She knew what he intended to do, and shyness brought with it a breath of sanity that made her push at his shoulders in an attempt to avoid the intimacies he was seeking, but the pressure of his mouth on hers increased with a flaming passion that sapped her strength. He eased himself away from her slightly, and she felt her dress sliding down to her waist. Her hands fluttered towards his wrists in a final, desperate attempt to stop him, but his fingers deftly unhooked the front catch of her bra, and he peeled the flimsy material away to cup her small breasts in the palms of his strong hands.

Everything stilled inside her for a moment, then her heart resumed its beat at a wilder pace, and she trembled with the force of the sharp, sweet pleasure he aroused when his sensitive fingers probed and caressed her hardened nipples. She was aware suddenly of a glowing sensuality in her body, and an alien desire that sent a tight, aching warmth rushing down into her loins when his mouth left hers to rake along her throat and down to her breast to complete the arousal his fingers had started.

A moan of pleasure passed her lips on a sigh, and her

hands were moving across his shoulders in a strangely convulsive movement to draw him closer as her body arched beneath his with a desire that had slipped beyond her control.

He lifted himself up on to his elbows, his breathing as ragged as her own, and his eyes, like smoky flames, devoured her flushed face and her pale breasts with the pink, hardened nipples. Shyness dimmed the glow of rapture, but deepened the flush on her cheeks, and a strange look entered his eyes.

'Revil?' She questioned that look in an anxious whisper, and his expression hardened to become set in that familiar mask of contempt that made her cringe inwardly with shame when he lifted himself away from her and got up.

'No, Alexa, don't tempt me with your beautiful body.' He spoke derisively over his shoulder, misconstruing the reason for her query. 'I'll take you when it suits me, and not before. The mood is not right tonight. Too many things have been said, and there's still too much anger in me to find pleasure in your body.'

So he wouldn't take her in anger. Alexa supposed she ought to appreciate the fact that he was showing her some consideration, but she was too sick with shame and self-disgust to appreciate anything at that moment. She fastened her bra with trembling fingers and zipped herself into her dress while his back was mercifully turned towards her. What on earth had possessed her to allow him those hitherto forbidden intimacies? she wondered angrily, combing her fingers through her untidy hair, and rising to retrieve her combs on the glass table.

'Take me home, please, Revil,' she said dully, slipping the combs into her purse, and he turned without looking at her to put on his jacket.

Revil drove her to her flat in silence, and he was so

aloof and unapproachable that she could scarcely believe what had happened in his penthouse. He unlocked the door to her flat, and she wondered whether he was going to leave her there without a word when he tipped her face up to his. His smoke-grey eyes probed hers in the dim passage light, and the breath seemed to still in her throat as she sustained his glance.

'It's been an enlightening evening.' He smiled twistedly, watching the flags of embarrassment rise in her cheeks. 'Perhaps, in time, I'll discover what it is that attracts me to someone who is so completely the opposite of what I believe a woman should be.'

He lowered his head to kiss her firmly but gently on the mouth, and he was gone before she had time to recover from her surprise.

Alexa had difficulty in falling asleep that night. She knew now that there was one sure way Revil could hurt her if he should choose to do so. He had proved quite conclusively that he was an experienced lover, and he had also proved that she was emotionally vulnerable where he was concerned. She had foolishly confessed that much to him by admitting that she had felt that same instant attraction three years ago, and she had no doubt that he was going to use that information to his own advantage. The attraction was still there. If she didn't place a guard on her heart it could very easily become something more profound, and he would have it within his power to hurt her more deeply than anyone else ever could.

Knowing this ought to have made it easier for her to prepare herself for the offensive, but Alexa had never before encountered a situation such as this, and she had no idea how she would deal with it. Something warned her, however, that the heart had a mind of its own, and she very much feared that she would find herself enmeshed in a tangled web of emotions from which there would be no escape.

Alexa was aware of being on the receiving end of strange, sidelong glances from the other models when she arrived at Bradstone Promotions two mornings later, and she was changing into her tights for their practice session when she discovered the reason for their curious looks.

'I said it would only be a matter of time, didn't I?' Lucille smiled, her voice lowered to keep their conversation private as she came up beside Alexa.

A bewildered look entered Alexa's clear, violet-blue eyes. 'What are you talking about, Lucille?'

'I'm talking about you and Revil Bradstone dining together at Santini's and ending off the evening *tête-à-tête* at his penthouse,' Lucille explained. 'The newspapers are full of it.'

'Oh!' Alexa exclaimed softly, her face whitening before going a deeper shade of pink.

She had expected this, and she had dreaded it, but it still came as a shock to her. She had now been publicly branded as the new woman in Revil Bradstone's life, and nothing she could say or do would ever make anyone believe they were not lovers.

'I know you've never taken kindly to people interfering in your personal life, but I have to tell you that I think you're looking for trouble,' Lucille warned, tying a scarf about her head to act as a sweat-band. 'I mean, you've never even had the briefest relationship with a man, and a girl like you simply won't stand a chance against a man as experienced as Revil Bradstone.'

Alexa knew what Lucille was trying to convey to her. Revil had already proved with what diabolical ease he could shatter her resistance, and it had resulted in two sleepless nights fearing what she had begun to realise would be inevitable. There had been one crazy moment when she had thought that she might actually welcome being possessed physically. He would then discover how wrongly he had judged her, and she would be free, but she knew also that the price she would have to pay for her freedom would be much too high. She would have lost not only her virginity, but her self-respect, and the latter was something which she knew she could not live without.

'I appreciate your concern, Lucille, but I'll manage.'

She *had* to manage, Alexa thought dismally when they followed the other girls out of the dressing-room, and this time she knew she would have to manage without Madame Véronique's assistance.

That was the start of a particularly exhausting day. Madame Véronique was in a strange mood, and it affected them all, including André Dacre. Nothing seemed to go right. If they were not slouching, then they were walking too fast, and Alexa developed a pounding headache which became progressively worse as the day wore on.

'That will be all for today, girls,' Madame announced at four-thirty that afternoon, and Alexa felt herself sagging mentally and physically with relief when Madame's dark eyes met hers across the room. 'I wish to see you in the office before you go, Alexa.'

'Uh-oh!' Lucille muttered softly behind Alexa. 'It sounds as if you're in for a lecture.'

Alexa cast a wary glance in her friend's direction before she followed Madame Véronique into the office she shared with André Dacre, and Madame uncharacteristically closed the door before she seated herself behind the desk and gestured Alexa into a chair.

'What is this I read in the newspaper, Alexa?'

Madame demanded without wasting time with platitudes. 'Is it true?'

It should not have come as a shock to Alexa that Madame had read the report in the newspaper, but somehow it did, and her tired, perspiration-drenched body went cold.

'Yes, it's true, Madame. I had dinner with Revil Bradstone two nights ago, and afterwards he took me to his penthouse, but I am not his new ... er ...'

'*Petite amie?*' Madame Véronique filled in distastefully when Alexa stumbled to an embarrassed halt. 'Do you not realise, *chérie*, that people who do not know you as I do will believe what they have read in the newspaper, and will think of you as his new woman?'

Alexa winced inwardly, but her gaze did not falter. 'I know what they will think, Madame.'

'And you do not care?' The query was rapped out incredulously.

'I care very much, Madame.'

'Then why do you allow yourself to be seen with this man?'

Alexa could not answer that truthfully, she was not quite sure of the answer herself. Perhaps it was her driving need to clear her name which had made her accept his invitation, and perhaps she would continue to see him in the hope of succeeding because, in some strange way, it mattered what he thought of her.

'I enjoy his company, Madame.'

'*Mon Dieu!*' Madame exploded, her dark gaze narrowing as she studied Alexa intently for several seconds. 'I assume you know that his sister was married to James Henderson?'

'Yes, I know.'

Madame Véronique's dark eyebrows rose a fraction. 'Does he know that *you* are the girl who was involved in that incident at the hotel?'

'Yes, he knows,' Alexa answered truthfully, shifting rather uncomfortably on the chair beneath Madame's penetrating dark gaze.

'I have heard that Revil Bradstone and his sister have always been very close.' Madame leaned forward in her chair, lacing her hands together on the blotter while she studied Alexa intently. 'Have you considered the possibility that he might be seeking revenge; that he might eventually make certain demands which will not only leave you hurt, but your reputation in ruins?'

Madame Véronique had hit on the truth so accurately that Alexa's composure was severely taxed in the effort to hide this from her mentor.

'I have considered that possibility, Madame,' Alexa replied with a serenity that did not come from within at that moment, and Madame sagged back in her chair with an incredulous look on her aristocratic features.

'I believe you are actually willing to take the chance that this man will treat you honourably.'

'I am willing to take that chance, Madame,' Alexa echoed, nursing her anguish privately.

She had no idea whether it was Revil's intention to treat her honourably. He was, at the moment, filled with too much of that anger he had mentioned the other evening, and until that anger subsided she could not attempt to predict his actions.

'Alexa, *chérie*, in many ways you are still as trusting as a child.' Madame's quiet voice invaded her frantic thoughts. 'Revil Bradstone has a reputation for being irresistible to women, and you, Alexa, will be like a lamb led innocently to the slaughter.'

'I can look after myself,' Alexa announced, looking into the doubtful eyes of the older woman. 'Please, Madame, don't worry about me.'

Alexa left the office a few moments later to see Revil walking towards her across the carpeted showroom, and

her heart quickened its pace nervously. This was the first
time she was seeing him since the night he had taken her
out to dinner, and a wave of heat surged into her cheeks
at the memory of what had occurred.

Smoke-grey eyes glinted mockingly when they paused
facing each other. His glance took in her flushed cheeks,
then raked the length of her body in the black leotard
and tights which left virtually nothing to the imagination, and her colour deepened with embarrassment
when his glance lingered longer than necessary on her
small, heaving breasts.

'I'll pick you up at seven this evening,' he said in a
cold, clipped voice. 'I've got tickets for the theatre, and
we'll have dinner afterwards.'

'Revil . . .' She raised a weary hand and his glance
sharpened at once on the shadows beneath her eyes. 'I'm
tired, and I really don't feel like going out this evening,'
she pleaded.

Did she imagine it, or did his expression soften slightly
when he raised a hand to finger a stray curl against her
temple?

'It's important that you accompany me to the theatre
this evening.' She stood immobile with surprise beneath
the oddly gentle touch of his fingers trailing fire down
her cheek to the base of her throat where her pulse was
throbbing erratically. 'I shan't keep you out later than I
have to,' he added persuasively.

Alexa nodded in agreement almost without thinking,
and a strange smile curved his sometimes cruel mouth
which left her staring curiously at his tall, broad-
shouldered frame when he strode away from her. What
was so important that she had to accompany Revil to the
theatre that evening?

CHAPTER FOUR

THE theatre lights were dimmed, and Alexa could feel her body grow taut as the curtain rose that opening night on the first act of a modern drama in which Carol Ross played the lead. Alexa had been dismayed when she had discovered this on their arrival at the theatre, but she had not dared to question Revil. It was none of her business why he had chosen to take her to a play in which his former girl-friend had the lead role, but she did wonder about it. He had said it was important that she accompany him, but she could not imagine of what importance her presence could be.

Carol Ross was a beautiful and talented actress, and the inflections in her clear, schooled voice added to the pathos of the role she was portraying. She was a brilliant performer, and Alexa, her tiredness temporarily forgotten, sat enthralled and almost oblivious of the man beside her until the curtain came down on the final act.

Alexa's participation in the applause was enthusiastic and spontaneously sincere, and she rose to her feet with everyone else to participate in the standing ovation Carol Ross deserved for her performance. 'She was magnificent! She's an absolutely outstanding actress!'

'Yes, outstanding,' Revil echoed drily, and Alexa glanced at him curiously when the lights finally came on in the theatre, but his stern features revealed nothing to her.

They joined the slow-moving throng up the aisle, and when they reached the lobby Revil drew her towards a door marked *Private*.

She cast a bewildered glance in his direction. 'Where are we going?'

'Wait and see,' he answered her curtly, his fingers tightening about her arm when she tried to draw back.

'Good evening, Mr Bradstone.' The uniformed doorkeeper smiled at Revil, and his gaze swivelled curiously in Alexa's direction as he raised his fingers to the peak of his braided cap in a respectful salute. 'It's almost like old times to have you coming back-stage after a show, sir.'

'Almost,' Revil agreed with a tight smile, his grip on Alexa's arm tightening rather than slackening. 'May we go in, Harry?'

'Certainly, sir.' The doorkeeper opened the door and stood aside for them to enter. 'There are reporters with Miss Ross at the moment, but I'm sure Miss Ross will be glad to see you ... and your lady, of course.'

The latter was added as a polite afterthought, but Alexa was afraid that her presence back-stage with Revil might have exactly the opposite effect on Carol Ross, and she wondered if she ought to prepare herself for an attempt to have her eyes clawed out.

Revil inclined his head briefly in answer to the doorkeeper's remark, and Alexa was ushered through the door and up the few steps that led to the dressing-rooms.

'Revil, I ... I don't think I should go with you,' Alexa whispered, her heart beating nervously in her throat at the prospect of meeting Carol Ross.

'You'd like to congratulate her on her performance, wouldn't you?' Revil demanded sharply, pausing in his stride to study her with a sardonic lift to his eyebrows.

'Yes, but——' She swallowed to remove the restriction in her throat. 'Under the circumstances I don't think it would be very kind of you to arrive at her dressing-room unannounced, and especially not with me.'

He looked down into violet-blue eyes that mirrored her deep concern, and a look of incredulity flashed across his handsome face before the cold, disbelieving mask once again shifted into place.

'Come on, we're wasting time,' he said, the sweep of his hand angry and impatient.

Revil knew his way about back-stage. The door to Carol Ross's small dressing-room stood open, and half a dozen reporters had crowded into it with their cameras and notebooks. The actress turned, her delight evident in her smiling features at the sight of Revil, and several surprised and speculative glances were suddenly directed at Revil and Alexa.

'Please, gentlemen, let that be all for tonight.' That very attractive and now familiar voice addressed the newsmen, and Carol Ross, her Titian-coloured hair spilling down to her shoulders, ushered them politely out of her dressing-room and gestured Revil and Alexa inside before she closed the door for privacy. '*Darling!*' the actress exclaimed warmly, looking even more beautiful without the layers of stage make-up as she stepped into Revil's arms for his fond embrace. 'Thank you for coming.'

'Have I ever missed an opening night?' he smiled, kissing her affectionately on the smooth cheek she proffered before he released her. 'Your performance, as usual, was magnificent, Carol.'

'Thank you, darling, and—no, don't tell me,' she stopped Revil when he was about to introduce Alexa, and clear green eyes met Alexa's with a steady regard that contained no sign of the venomous jealousy Alexa had expected. 'The newspaper photograph didn't do you justice, my dear,' she said at length, a friendly smile lifting the corners of her full, sensuous mouth. 'It's Alexa Drew, isn't it?'

'That's correct,' Alexa replied, forcing her lips into an answering smile.

'Did you enjoy the play?' Carol questioned Alexa.

'It was a marvellous play, and your performance was absolutely outstanding.' She repeated her earlier statement to Revil.

'It's kind of you to say so.' She continued to study Alexa with an oddly thoughtful expression in her eyes, then she turned and gestured expressively with her hands. 'Grab a chair and sit down, won't you?'

'We can't, I'm afraid,' Revil declined Carol's invitation. 'Alexa and I are dining out, and she needs to have an early night.'

'What a pity.' An expression, fleeting but revealing, entered Carol Ross's eyes. She was in love with Revil, and that, Alexa realised with sudden clarity, was the reason why this woman's relationship with Revil had ended. 'Oh, well, perhaps we'll get together at some future date,' the actress shrugged with affected casualness.

'You can count on that,' Revil agreed, taking Alexa's arm and drawing her towards the door, but Carol Ross raised a detaining hand, and directed her green gaze at Alexa.

'Before you go, darling, I think I ought to give you a word of advice.' She addressed Alexa with a mixture of humour and sadness in her smile. 'Don't fall in love with this man. He's wonderfully warm and generous, and I shall always adore him, but when it comes to love he has a heart of stone, as his name suggests.'

'Don't be fooled by Alexa's appearance, Carol.' Revil smiled twistedly, the warmth leaving his eyes when his gaze swept down the length of Alexa's slender, elegantly clad body. 'Underneath this angelic exterior,' he gestured disparagingly with his hand, 'there lurks a heart that's harder than my own.'

Alexa stood as if turned to stone. If Revil had wanted to insult and humiliate her, then he could not have chosen a better place, or a better time. To bring her face to face with the woman who had shared the intimate side of his life for more than a year had been cruel and embarrassing, but the hurt he had inflicted with his remarks was like a piercing stab through her heart which she could not find an explanation for at that moment.

'Revil!' Carol Ross's beautiful features were etched in shock and disbelief. 'I don't know you like this!'

'No,' he agreed in a cold, clipped voice, 'but then neither do you know Alexa.'

An odd compassion flickered in Carol Ross's green eyes, but it was replaced by cynical amusement when her gaze rested on Alexa's pale face. It seemed as if, for the briefest second, they shared each other's thoughts with a mutual understanding, then Carol Ross turned to face Revil with a strangely triumphant glitter in her eyes.

'Take heed you find not that you do not seek, my dear Revil,' she warned softly.

'Quoting proverbs at me again, are you?' he mocked her.

'Yes, I am,' Carol laughed softly, her green silken robe dragging on the floor behind her when she saw them to the door, 'and I happen to think this one is very appropriate for the occasion.'

They left the theatre via a side entrance, and drove to the restaurant in silence. The reporters were waiting outside Santini's with their cameras and their probing, intimate queries, but Alexa was too tired to pay much attention to what was being said. The restaurant was busy even at that time of the evening and, when Alexa sat sipping her wine, she realised how exhausted she actually was. Caution was not something she could apply at a time like that, and the forbidden queries simply spilled from her lips.

'Why did you take me to see that particular play, and why did you insist on taking me back-stage to meet Carol Ross?'

There was a hint of self-satisfaction in Revil's humorous smile. 'There are always reporters in attendance on the opening night of a play, and especially when Carol is acting in it.'

'And you wanted the members of the press to see the three of us together on friendly terms because you still care enough for Carol Ross to want to squash that unkind rumour of attempted suicide which is in circulation,' she added, the pain he had inflicted earlier forgotten, and her admiration and respect growing as she glimpsed the real man behind the cold, contemptuous mask she found herself confronted with at times.

'Clever girl!' Revil mocked her. 'I didn't credit you with that much intuition, but it appears you do have a thinking brain in that beautiful head of yours after all.'

He was making use of every despicable method to hurt her, inflicting pain which was undeserved, and in a rare flash of anger she found the courage to say the things she would never have said under normal circumstances.

'I credited you with a brilliant, perceptive mind, but you have disappointed me,' she berated him, a sharp edge to her usually calm, controlled voice. 'You're more gullible than most and, added to that, you're stubborn, self-righteous, and egotistical. You think you have all the answers, and you play at being God, but I can only pity you.'

'You know you're guilty of the accusations I have made, and it's only natural to lash out when you find yourself in a tight corner,' he incorrectly interpreted her outburst, burdening her with that hateful feeling of helpless frustration.

'I'm guilty of having compassion and lending a sympathetic ear to a man who did not deserve it,' she defended herself. 'I'm guilty of showing concern, and of offering my assistance when I was falsely led to believe that it was needed, but I'm *not* guilty of the vile accusations you have made.'

Her emphatic and impassioned statement ignited a flicker of doubt in his eyes before they narrowed perceptibly, and his mouth tightened into a thin, angry line. 'If I'm to believe you, then I must also believe that my sister lied to me, and that what I saw was merely an innocent, terrified girl running away from a situation which had horrified her.'

'I'm not making accusations, but you can believe me, Revil, because I'm telling you the truth.'

They faced each other across the table in a silence which was tense and strained, and the look of uncertainty on Revil's handsome features was not only touching, it made him suddenly appear so very human.

'God knows I'm tempted to believe you,' Revil growled, leaning towards her to capture her hand in his. 'When I look at you I see honesty and innocence, but there's a demon inside me that says it could be a carefully contrived act to deceive me, and I'm once again forced to believe that my sister spoke the truth about what she had seen when she entered that hotel room that night.'

Alexa admired his loyalty to his sister, but she did not want to be in Wilma Henderson's shoes when Revil finally discovered the truth for himself.

'What did your sister see?' Alexa heard herself asking,

and a tortured expression flashed across Revil's face before his sensuous mouth twisted in a smile of derision which she felt was not entirely directed at her.

'Do you really need me to tell you?' he demanded, releasing her hand abruptly, and Alexa nodded slowly.

'I would very much like to hear her version.'

A savage expression glittered in his eyes, and she swallowed down the remainder of her wine in one quick gulp to steady the nerves fluttering at the pit of her stomach.

'She found you in James's arms, partially naked, and making no visible attempt to repulse him.'

The lights in the restaurant dipped and swayed. Oh, Lord, she had had too much wine on an empty stomach, or perhaps this light-headedness had been brought on by hearing Revil recite what his sister had told him. A new thought came to mind as her dizzy world slowly righted itself. Was it possible that Wilma Henderson truly believed she had spoken the truth, because she had *wanted* to find a woman in her husband's arms that night? Horrible thought! Whatever had made her think of it? Wilma Henderson had lied for some obscure reason, and she had known that her brother would believe her implicitly.

'Does your sister live in Johannesburg?'

'Yes, but she's away at the moment on a two-month visit to friends on the Greek Isles.'

How very convenient that she isn't here when she's needed! Alexa wanted to say, but the query in Revil's gaze made her say instead, 'I was merely curious.'

What had she hoped to gain by asking a question like that? she wondered crossly. Had she hoped that she might be able to confront Wilma and force her somehow to reveal the truth?

Their meal was served, and Alexa stared at her sirloin

steak with no particular desire to eat it. It was superbly prepared, and garnished with her favourite mushroom sauce, but the thought of eating seemed to nauseate her. Revil cut into his T-bone steak, enjoying it, and oblivious of the fact that Alexa was merely nibbling at her food to be polite.

Alexa studied him unobtrusively while he ate. He was a good-looking man with a brilliant mind which had placed him in a powerful position in the field of advertising, and he was not the type of man any woman would meet and forget lightly. She regretted some of the things she had accused him of, and it was true that she had lashed out at him because she had found herself in a tight corner, but he was wrong in thinking that she had been motivated by guilt. If only he would believe her! She could not explain why, but it was important to her that he believed her. She did not want him to think of her as a woman without morals; she wanted him to . . .!

Startled, Alexa reined in her wayward thoughts, and found herself confronted by Revil's frowning, smoke-grey glance across the table. Her heart seemed to somersault in her breast with a knowledge which she found too frightening to dwell on, and she fastidiously shut it out of her mind.

'You're not eating,' Revil accused.

He had nice hands; strong, long-fingered hands that could arouse the most incredible emotions as well as inflict pain. What would it feel like to have those hands stroking her body with love as the motive, rather than with the intention to punish? She trembled, and her pulse rate quickened to leave her slightly breathless.

'I'm not very hungry, and I'd like to go home,' she said bluntly, not daring to look at him.

Dear God, she *had* to go home! She was beginning to

think things and feel things which could only cause her more pain.

Alexa expected Revil to object, but he signalled the waiter to ask for the bill, and they left the restaurant almost immediately.

'Are you ill?' Revil questioned her unexpectedly when they drove through the well-lit city streets.

'No, I'm not,' she answered abruptly, staring straight ahead of her, and wishing her heart would stop racing at such a suffocating pace.

'You were quite pale in the restaurant.'

Oh, God! she groaned inwardly. Please let it be tiredness that deranged me temporarily to think and feel the way I did!

'Don't concern yourself, Revil,' she said with unaccustomed sarcasm. 'I'm not about to become ill to rob you of the opportunity to have your revenge.'

He pulled the car into a computer distrubution company's loading zone, and his features were etched in fury in the dashboard light when he turned to face her.

'I'm not an insensitive, sadistic monster,' he rebuked her harshly. 'I admit that three years of accumulated anger might have made me appear that way when you came to my office on Madame Véronique's behalf, but I've had time to cool down since then.'

Alexa felt her heart lurch with hope in her breast. 'Does that mean you've relinquished the idea of taking your revenge?'

'Oh, no, Alexa,' he smiled twistedly. 'I shall be digging relentlessly beneath the surface of your angelic mask until I know the truth, and then, if it is necessary, I shall have my revenge.'

Alexa hovered somewhere between relief and fear. If she had achieved nothing else, then she had at least succeeded in sowing a tiny seed of doubt, but he would dig relentlessly until he uncovered the truth, he had said, and she knew somehow that it was going to be a long, painful process for both of them.

'Please take me home, Revil,' she pleaded. 'I'm exhausted and I have a pounding headache.'

Revil took her home as she had requested, but he did not leave her at her door as she had expected. One glance at her white, pinched face made him follow her inside, and he took charge of the situation, ordering her in an authoritative manner to undress and get into bed. She did not have the energy left to protest, or wonder what he was up to, and she obeyed him in silence.

The muscles in her neck and shoulders were bunched into aching knots, and she was sitting up in bed, rubbing the back of her neck with a grimace on her face, when Revil tapped sharply on her door. He was inside her bedroom and approaching her bed with a glass of milk in his hand, and the flickering light in his smoke-grey eyes told her that he had glimpsed her small, taut breasts through her flimsy nightie during those startled seconds before she had lowered her hands to jerk up the blankets as a shield.

He raised an amused eyebrow, and nudged her shoulder when he had put down the glass of milk. 'Sit that way so I can move in behind you.'

'What——'

'Don't ask questions, just do as I say,' he interrupted her sternly, taking off his black evening jacket and flinging it across the foot of the bed, and once again she found herself obeying him.

Revil seated himself behind her, his hard thigh pressing against her hip as he brushed her hair forward over her shoulders, and her nerves jolted when she felt his hands against her skin where exhaustion had knotted her muscles.

'Relax,' he instructed, his strong fingers seeking and finding those painful muscles to massage and knead them repeatedly until the pain of tension subsided and they became pliable beneath his therapeutic manipulations.

Her eyes were closed, relief bringing a smile of contentment to her lips and, dropping her guard, she leaned back against Revil to relax comfortably against his solid chest.

'Is this an invitation for a more intimate form of therapy?' he murmured throatily in her ear while his arms went about her and brushed unintentionally but excitingly against her breasts, and she was too pleasantly relaxed to be alarmed by the physical reaction he aroused.

'You know it isn't,' she protested on a sigh.

'I'm not so sure of that,' he contradicted her with a soft, devilish laugh, his hands on her shoulders and his fingers sliding in a tantalising caress beneath the lacy straps of her nightie. 'What I am sure of at the moment is that you're genuinely too exhausted to know exactly what you're doing, and I may be a heel at times, but I have no intention of taking advantage of a situation such as this.'

He released her abruptly and got up to pass her the milk he had poured for her, and she felt strangely bereft without his arms about her.

'Why are you being so extraordinarily kind to me, Revil?' she questioned him, observing him curiously over the rim of the glass while he shrugged himself into his evening jacket.

'I wish I knew.' His smile was twisted and the bedside light accentuated the strange glitter in his eyes when he stood beside her bed looking down at her thoughtfully.

'Perhaps it's a case of fattening up the turkey before it has to be slaughtered.'

'Is there going to be a slaughter?' she asked, holding her breath mentally while she continued to observe him through a veil of silken, silvery hair, and that cold, impenetrable mask shifted back into place to send a shiver of apprehension racing up her spine.

'That depends on the final analysis.' His voice had been brusque as if they had been discussing one of his advertising projects, and he turned towards the door, depriving her of the opportunity to read his expression. 'I'll put the latch on the door as I leave.'

Alexa emptied the glass of milk after Revil had left, but she lay for a long time in the darkness without being able to fall asleep, and her thoughts were centred solely on Revil.

He could be so agonisingly cruel, and yet he could be kind when the necessity arose. He could listen to reason, but he could also be totally unrelenting. She admired his loyalty to his sister, but she could also sense an inner turmoil beneath that granite-hard exterior. What was it he had said? If he was to believe her, then he also had to believe that his sister had lied to him. Carol Ross had said that Revil was wonderfully warm and generous, but his sister's poisonous lies had robbed Alexa of the opportunity to experience that warm generosity to the full, and she could almost hate Wilma Henderson for that.

Don't fall in love with this man, Carol Ross had warned. He has a heart of stone as his name suggests.

That was sound advice from someone who had acquainted herself with the painful consequences of falling in love with a man who could never love her in return. Carol Ross's warning had, however, been unnecessary. Alexa had known from the start that she must never, *ever* be foolish enough to fall in love with

Revil Bradstone unless she was prepared to spend the
rest of her life mourning the fact that she could never
have him. He could be kind and warm and generous, she
had had a taste of that humane side of him this evening,
and during her own analysis of Revil's character she had
made the surprising discovery that there was a caring
soul beneath that rock-hard exterior which he presented
to her at times. She could not condemn him entirely for
what he believed of her; she was convinced that, if their
positions had been reversed, she might have felt the
same, and for this reason she could find it in her own
generous, compassionate heart to understand and
forgive him.

She would have to take care, she warned herself.
There was no sense in denying that she was wildly
attracted to Revil despite his sometimes hateful and
contemptuous manner towards her, but to spend time
listing his endearing qualities could prove fatal for her
peace of mind.

Alexa saw Revil only briefly during the following week
when, on two occasions, he put in a brief appearance at
the rehearsals, but he nevertheless succeeded in making
his presence felt, and even at a distance she could feel
those smoke-grey eyes lingering on her body with a
piercing intensity which left her with the curious
sensation that he had touched her physically.

'We shall have to decide which one of the girls will
model the wedding-gown,' André Dacre announced one
morning before the final dress-rehearsals began, and a
murmur of excitement rose amongst the models. 'I want
someone who will complement the sweet, pure, and
youthful innocence of my design.'

'May I make a suggestion?' a deep and familiar voice
queried unexpectedly, and Alexa felt her treacherous

heart quicken its pace at the sight of the tall, broad-shouldered man walking towards them across the showroom floor.

Revil's presence commanded everyone's attention, and André Dacre, great man though he was in his own field, turned to Revil with obvious respect for the chairman of Bradstone's professional guidance.

'I shall welcome whatever suggestion you care to make,' the brilliant designer declared readily when Revil joined him and Madame Véronique at the far end of the platform.

Revil thrust his hands into his pockets and rocked slightly on his heels while his narrowed, smoke-grey glance skimmed over the models grouped together at the opposite end of the platform, and Alexa felt a terrible apprehension gripping her insides when his eyes met hers.

'I can't think of anyone who will succeed in projecting the image you want better than Alexa Drew,' Revil voiced his opinion, and Alexa stiffened, incapable of deciding whether it was sincerity or contemptuous mockery which had prompted his statement.

Oh, God! If only Revil had not used the words 'projecting an image'! she thought despairingly.

'An excellent choice, *monsieur*,' Madame Véronique agreed, her aristocratic features glowing. 'Alexa, *chérie*, come forward, *s'il vous plaît*.'

It was fortunate, perhaps, that there was no rivalry between Alexa and the rest of the models, and their encouraging murmurs gave her the strength she needed to walk down the length of the platform in her tights and leotard while three pairs of eyes observed her with varying expressions.

'Take a good look, André,' Revil was saying, removing one hand from his pocket to make a sweeping gesture in Alexa's direction. 'What you see there is a sweetness, an almost childlike purity, and a youthful innocence rolled into one feminine package. A white wedding-gown has been looked upon through the ages as a symbol of virginity, and Alexa will project that image to perfection.'

There was a deliberate sting to Revil's complimentary remarks, but no one appeared to notice it except Alexa, and she somehow succeeded in wearing a mask of calmness while her insides were in fierce revolt.

'I see what you mean, Revil. I do indeed.' André Dacre smiled up at Alexa, his face transformed as if he could actually see her in the wedding-gown he had created. 'You have made an excellent choice. She has all the qualities I wanted, and more.'

'Ah, yes, she possesses more qualities than we'll ever guess,' Revil echoed, his compelling glance capturing Alexa's. 'I warned you that I would dig until I knew the truth, didn't I?' he seemed to be saying to her before he addressed the couturier once again. 'When Alexa is wearing your wedding-gown she will steal the show and, if she's lucky, she might even succeed in arousing a flutter in the hearts of a few staid married men.'

His remark aroused a titter of laughter, but Alexa was not laughing. She knew what he was referring to; she was aware of the hidden accusation which his loyalty to his sister had compelled him to make, and her heart wept silently.

André Dacre turned to Alexa, and gestured her down off the platform almost impatiently. 'We will start with the fittings at once,' he said, his voice vibrating with excitement, then he turned towards Madame Véronique and asked almost as an afterthought, 'Can you spare Alexa this morning, Madame?'

'But of course, *monsieur*,' Madame replied accommodatingly, and Alexa had one last glimpse of Revil's broad, formidable back which he had turned resolutely towards her before she was whisked off to André Dacre's work-room.

'Revil has a discerning eye where women are concerned,' the designer remarked when she stood before him draped in white satin panels which had been pinned and tacked together temporarily. 'Or perhaps his knowledge stems from a personal interest in you?' André Dacre added with a wicked gleam in his dark eyes.

'I wouldn't know, Mr Dacre,' Alexa responded stiffly.

'Oh, come now, Alexa!' he laughed, taking in a dart and pinning it to fit her slender figure. 'You may talk freely with me while we work.'

'We may talk freely, Mr Dacre,' Alexa agreed warily, 'but not about Revil Bradstone.'

'Ah, you wish to keep your relationship with him private, but I have noticed that the press will not allow this,' he smiled wryly, popping pins between his compressed lips.

'Do you believe everything that is printed in the newspapers?' she asked curiously, and with a great deal of caution.

'If you're asking me whether I believe the newspaper report that you're Revil Bradstone's new live-in lady-friend, then the answer is *no*,' André Dacre announced, removing the pins from between his lips, and stepping back to regard her with a faint smile hovering about his mouth. 'Revil is not the only one who possesses a discerning eye. You *are* sweet and pure and innocent, and perhaps that explains the glint of mockery I saw in his eyes when he suggested you should model the wedding-gown.'

Alexa stared at him speechlessly for a moment, then a warmth flooded her cold heart which almost succeeded in bringing tears to her eyes. 'Thank you, Mr Dacre.'

He raised a comical eyebrow. 'Why are you thanking me?'

'For not being so ready to believe the worst of me,' Alexa answered him quietly and simply, and his warm brown eyes smiled into hers for a moment before he adopted a stern expression.

'Don't slouch, Alexa!' he instructed in a businesslike voice. 'How am I expected to make the necessary adjustments if you slouch like a tired animal!'

Alexa smiled as she straightened her shoulders and stood like the required statue while he pinned and tacked where necessary, but there was a trace of sadness in her smile. If only Revil could bring himself to believe in her innocence the way André Dacre had done.

CHAPTER FIVE

'TAKE the afternoon off and rest this weekend,' Madame had instructed when they stopped for lunch the Friday. 'As from Monday you will all be working at twice the usual pace.'

Alexa had known what that meant. When Madame Véronique said they would be working at 'twice the usual pace', it meant exactly that. They would work until they were almost ready to drop, and this brief reprieve ought to be used to its best advantage. That was why Alexa had gone home to her one-bedroomed flat to linger for almost half an hour in a hot bath until the tiredness had eased out of her aching muscles. She put on an old pair of slacks and a thick, baggy sweater, and settled down comfortably on the sofa with a good book she had been anxious to read for some time, but she had barely read five pages when the doorbell rang.

She sat up with a start, her body tensing, and her heart pounding against her ribs. Some hidden instinct warned her that it would be Revil Bradstone and, when the doorbell rang persistently a second time, she knew that she dared not ignore it.

'Pack a bag,' Revil instructed her dictatorially seconds later when he strode into her flat without waiting for an invitation. 'You're coming with me for the weekend.'

Alexa stiffened with resentment, but her senses responded to his masculine appeal as her mind registered the blue denims spanning tightly across his muscled thighs, and the black woollen sweater which accentuated the width of his powerful shoulders.

'I've no intention of going anywhere with you!' she protested hotly, alarmed by the weakness surging into her limbs and, despite the steely glint in his eyes, she added, 'You have no right to barge in here, and neither have you the right to impose your wishes on me.'

'I need a break away from the city, and so do you, and we're simply wasting time by arguing, Alexa.' He glanced at the gold watch strapped to his strong wrist and added curtly, 'We have a plane to catch in less than two hours, and I suggest you don't pack anything fancy. Slacks and cool blouses will do.'

He had a nerve! His arrogance had shattered her usually calm disposition, but instead she was beginning to like the idea of a weekend away from Johannesburg. Would she be safe alone with Revil? She did not think so. He could be cruel as well as kind, but at that particular moment the hard, unrelenting line of his jaw told her that she really had very little choice in the matter. If she refused to accompany him he was quite capable of taking her with him by force, and she didn't relish the thought of a humiliating scene.

'May I know where we're going?' she demanded not so meekly. If he was going to whisk her off somewhere for the weekend, then she had a right to know their eventual destination. Hadn't she?

'We're going to the Izilwane Game Park,' he enlightened her with surprising tolerance, taking her by the shoulders and spinning her round to face her bedroom door before he gave her a gentle shove in that direction. 'Now, get cracking, we haven't got all day.'

Alexa took down her weekend bag and flung a few pairs of slacks and blouses into it along with her underwear and toiletries. She could sense Revil moving about in her small lounge, his footsteps muted as he paced the carpeted floor impatiently, and it heightened her nervousness. She checked her bag, making sure that she had not forgotten anything, and fifteen minutes later they were speeding towards the airport in his Jaguar.

A twin-engined Cessna stood fuelled and waiting, and the pilot was making a few last-minute checks when they approached him across the tarmac. He raised his hand in a casual salute to Revil, grinned at Alexa in a way that sent the blood rushing into her cheeks, and stored their bags in the luggage compartment before they got into the Cessna and strapped themselves into their seats.

Alexa had never flown in a small aeroplane before, and she was noticeably nervous, but Revil was unaware of how she felt at that moment. He was checking the contents of his briefcase, and he made a quick study of a sheaf of papers before he returned it to his case and snapped the lid shut.

The pilot was speaking to the control tower, starting up the engines while he waited for instructions, and Alexa could feel the vibrations beneath her. She leaned back in her seat and tried to relax as they taxied slowly towards the runway. A Boeing took off, another came in to land, and then they were moving forward on to the runway. The pilot received his final instructions from the tower, the engines started revving at a terrifying pace, and seconds later they were moving forward at a speed which made Alexa catch her breath. She closed her eyes, experienced a sinking feeling, and when she opened her eyes again they were airborne.

'That wasn't so bad, was it?' Revil mocked her, raising his voice above the loud droning of the Cessna's engines.

'No, it wasn't,' she smiled self-consciously, embarrassed to discover that he had noticed her nervousness, and she hastily changed the subject. 'I've never heard of the Izilwane Game Park.'

'It's privately owned and still comparatively new,' Revil explained, the mockery leaving his smoke-grey eyes. 'Byron Rockford started this pet project of his about a year ago, and we're handling the promotional side of it for him.'

'Is that the reason for this weekend trip to Izilwane?'

'That's one of the reasons,' Revil smiled, the sensuous curve of his mouth sending a wave of warmth into her cheeks, and she looked away quickly, too afraid to ask what the other reasons were.

It was a clear day for flying, and Alexa settled back in her seat in an attempt to enjoy the flight despite those little stabs of anxiety.

Pretoria lay stretched out below them, its tree-lined streets and the Union Buildings with their magnificently terraced gardens a clearly visible landmark, but shortly afterwards they were flying over tobacco plantations and fruit orchards where hills dipped into lush, green valleys through which tributaries of the Limpopo flowed.

The scene below her changed rapidly and excitingly, and she had almost succeeded in forgetting about Revil when his hand touched her shoulder, making her jump and turn in her seat to see him pointing straight ahead.

'That's the Soutpansberg mountain range ahead of us, and beyond that it's bushveld country, or baobab country as some people call it,' he enlightened her, and she felt his eyes resting on her intently while she glanced in the direction he had pointed. 'Have you ever been this far north before?'

'No, never,' she admitted, shaking her head, and her glance was drawn to his as if by a magnet.

His gaze was intent upon her face, taking in her

heightened colour and the sparkle in her violet-blue eyes which stemmed from an inner excitement. She looked, for a moment, like a child embarking on an adventure, and Revil's stern mouth relaxed in a smile that had a devastating effect on Alexa. Her breath locked in her throat, her pulse rate quickened, and a trembling warmth rose from deep inside her that made her lips quiver into an answering smile.

'If you continue looking at me like that, then I'm going to kiss you,' Revil warned and, before she could avoid it, he was doing exactly that.

His hand was at the nape of her neck, drawing her towards him across the narrow aisle between their seats, and his hard mouth settled on hers to extract a response that left her shaken and trembling visibly. It had been a brief kiss, but it had proved to her once again how helpless she would be if he chose to make love to her as part of his vengeful punishment.

Revil's smile was mocking, as if he had read her thoughts, and she turned her head away angrily to look out of the window. *Damn him*! Did he have to make her feel as if she had been robbed of every scrap of privacy?

It took a tremendous effort to calm the beat of her heart, and it helped considerably to focus her attention on the landscape beneath her while she fought to regain her composure.

The northern Transvaal was, as Revil had informed her earlier, bushveld country. It was rugged and beautiful, and baobab trees were in abundance, looking oddly like trees which had been planted upside down with their roots reaching up into the sky. The pilot began the descent and, as he did so, she glimpsed a picturesque town nestling at the foot of the Soutpansberg mountains.

'We're flying over Louisville,' the pilot informed

them, 'and we'll be landing at the Izilwane Game Park in about five minutes, so make sure that your seat-belts are secure.'

Alexa glanced at her watch. Four-thirty. The flight had gone so quickly that she found it almost impossible to believe that it had taken them an hour and thirty minutes to reach their destination.

This was also cattle country, Alexa discovered to her delight when she stared out of the window and caught her first glimpse of the well-known Afrikander breed of cattle with their long horns, and the familiar hump above their shoulders. Their majestic, golden-brown bodies glistened in the sunlight where they grazed in the vast camps, and their muscles rippled as they moved about amongst the acacia trees.

The pilot had reduced speed to fly low over the game park north of Louisville, and in the slanting afternoon sun she could see zebras and various types of buck gathered together to drink water at the edge of a large dam. Alexa had never been to a game park before. Her heart started bouncing with excitement, and she hoped there would be time during the weekend to see some of the animals at closer range.

The trees parted some distance up ahead of them, clearly defining the landing strip which seemed to lie shimmering in the heat, and the plane lost height swiftly, touching down with a slight bump, the engines slowing and the flaps down to break their speed. The pilot brought the plane to a halt in a cloud of dust, turned it, and taxied back the way they had come to where a dusty Land Rover was parked along the side of the gravel runway.

The Cessna stopped at last, the engines were cut, and seconds later Revil was helping Alexa down on to solid ground. The silence, the heat, and the wild smell of the

bush rushed up to envelop her, but she barely had time
to take it in while Revil propelled her towards the
waiting Land Rover from which a giant of a man in
khaki trousers and safari-jacket emerged to welcome
them.

'You're right on time,' he said, his rugged features
creasing into a smile and the sun adding a coppery sheen
to his dark hair as his large hand gripped Revil's. 'It was
good of you to come at such short notice, Revil.'

'You should know that any excuse is good enough for
me to get away from the city for a while,' Revil laughed
shortly, his stern features relaxed in a way that made
Alexa's heart quicken, then he turned and, taking her
arm, propelled her forward once again. 'This is Alexa
Drew. Alexa, I'd like you to meet a very old friend of
mine, Byron Rockford.'

'Revil's making it sound as if we're both in our
dotage,' Byron Rockford laughed softly, his laughter like
the deep, distant roll of thunder as he extended a hand
towards Alexa, and she responded with an answering
smile as her small hand disappeared briefly in his firm
clasp.

'I'm pleased to meet you, Mr Rockford.'

'Likewise,' he grinned, his tawny gaze appreciative as
it skipped over her. 'And the name's Byron. We don't
stand on ceremony here.'

The pilot had deposited their luggage in the Land
Rover and, after a few brief words with Revil, he
returned to the Cessna.

'Shall we go?' Byron suggested, and moments later
Alexa was seated in the back of the Land Rover as it
bumped across the uneven track winding through the
trees and the tall grass towards the camp.

Revil sat up front with Byron. They were discussing
the new additions to the camp, but Alexa wasn't

listening. Her eyes were searching for signs of animal life, and her heart almost leapt into her throat when Byron slowed down as they passed a herd of long-necked giraffe browsing amongst the trees.

'I have twelve thousand acres of land here, and I've stocked it with everything except elephant and lion,' Byron was explaining to Revil when the Land Rover began to pick up speed. 'Elephant I can forget about since it would cost too much to reinforce the fencing, but I intend to introduce lion into the park during the next year or two.'

'How do the farmers in the district feel about that?' Revil questioned him.

'They're not very happy about it, but neither do they object.' His deep-throated laughter rumbled through the interior of the Land Rover. 'Their attitude is very much a case of "we don't mind, as long as you keep your animals where they belong".'

'Is there any chance of them getting through on to the farms?' Alexa risked voicing her own query.

'Not a chance.' Byron's tawny eyes smiled at her in the rear-view mirror. 'The only way the animals could get out of the park would be if someone cuts through the high fence surrounding it, and I don't have any fears of that at the moment.'

The camp lay up ahead of them, and the gates were opened by two uniformed men. Byron raised his hand in a brief salute as the Land Rover shot past the guards with a cloud of dust billowing up behind it, and he drove directly towards one of the larger, thatch-roofed bungalows nestling against the side of the hill amongst the shady mopani trees.

'We'll have something cool to drink here at my place, and afterwards I'll take you on a quick tour of the camp to show you the improvements we've made since your last visit.' Byron addressed Revil, but his brief glance in Alexa's direction when he parked his Land Rover along the side of the bungalow told her that she was included in that invitation to tour the camp. 'Leave your bags in the Land Rover,' he instructed when they got out. 'They'll be taken care of.'

Alexa felt dusty and hot as they followed Byron Rockford on to the shady and cool *stoep* along the front of his thatch-roofed bungalow, and Revil's mocking glance made her feel considerably worse. Byron gestured towards the cane chairs on his *stoep*, and they had barely seated themselves when a servant appeared as if on cue with a tray containing ice-cold beers and a jug of fruit juice.

'What can I offer you, Alexa?' Byron smiled at her, gesturing towards the tray which had been placed on a table at his elbow. 'Beer, or fruit juice?'

'I'll have a fruit juice, thank you,' Alexa replied, her throat suddenly as dry as the dust clinging to her sandalled feet, and she welcomed the sound of the ice clinking in the glass which was handed to her.

The men snapped open their beer cans and drank as thirstily as Alexa drank her fruit juice. She was surrounded once again by silence; a silence which was broken only by the sound of bird-song in the trees shading the bungalow. It was a silence that induced a blessed calmness into her tense body, and she felt herself relax slowly while she listened without paying attention to the low rumble of Revil and Byron Rockford's voices in conversation.

A telephone rang shrilly inside the bungalow. It was a modern commodity which seemed out of place in such serene and tranquil surroundings, and Byron excused himself hastily to answer it, but he returned a few seconds later with an apologetic expression on his rugged face.

'We've got a problem up at the water plant,' he explained. 'It means, I'm afraid, that we'll have to postpone that promised tour of the camp until the morning, but please help yourselves to another drink if you wish, and my houseboy will show you to your bungalow when you're ready.' He smiled ruefully. 'See you both later.'

Bungalow? The word stabbed through Alexa's wary mind as she watched Byron Rockford striding away up the hill. He had used the word in the singular, but surely he had meant *bungalows*? One for Revil, and one for herself? *Don't be silly*! she rebuked herself when that gnawing fear made her body feel cold and clammy. *Don't let your imagination run away with you*!

The silence, pleasant though it had been, was becoming rather awkward now that Alexa found herself alone with Revil who was relaxing in his chair with his long legs stretched out in front of him. He was as tall as Byron Rockford, but not quite as hefty and, when his grey glance met hers curiously, she said the first thing that came to mind in an attempt to cover up her embarrassment at being caught staring.

'I'm actually surprised Byron didn't find it strange that I accompanied you on this trip instead of one of your staff . . . like your secretary, for instance.'

Revil raised an amused, faintly sardonic eyebrow. 'I don't require the services of a secretary on these trips, and I can assure you that Byron doesn't find it strange at all that I decided to bring a woman along for the ride.'

Alexa wondered if she looked quite as startled as she felt. 'You've done this before?'

'Several times during the past year,' he admitted without a trace of embarrassment, offering her another

drink which she refused, and helping himself to a second
beer.

'I presume you brought Carol Ross?' she probed
daringly, watching him snap open the can and take a
long, thirsty drink before he answered her.

'I didn't necessarily always bring Carol.'

Alexa drew a controlled but angry breath. 'I must say
you're a master at pointing a finger at others while your
own reputation leaves much to be desired.'

'There is a difference, if you'd care to think about it.'
He smiled derisively, his eyes suddenly as cold as the ice
tinkling in her empty glass when she leaned forward in
her chair to place it in the tray. 'The women I have
known have all been unattached, and they have all been
adept at playing the same game I do.'

'And what game is that?' she asked unnecessarily.

'It's a game which excludes marriage, and which
leaves me, as well as the lady in question, free to come
and go as we please.'

'No ties, no responsibilities,' she interpreted his
remark cynically, and not without a certain amount of
pain. 'That's a shallow game, and rather cowardly, I
think.'

'You're pretty good at pointing a finger yourself,' he
accused, his deep voice harsh and biting. 'What could be
more shallow and cowardly than the game you play,
Alexa, and you have played it callously with a total lack
of concern for the people whose lives you've ruined.'

She knew only too well the futility of defending
herself. It seemed as if nothing she could say, or do,
would ever change his opinion of her, and yet she could
not prevent herself from making the attempt. 'I have
never deliberately done anything to hurt anyone, and I
wish you'd believe that I'm not guilty of ruining your
sister's life, or that of her husband.'

'Oh, really?'

His mockery heightened her frustration to the point of anger. She would have liked nothing better than to lash out at him verbally and physically, but this violent and uncharacteristic desire frightened her, and she drew a deep, steadying breath to calm herself.

'I've told you before that what happened was not my fault,' she protested with a quiet sincerity which he was determined to ignore.

'Your uncle and aunt wouldn't agree with you.' He seemed to take a callous delight in stabbing a cruel finger into a wound which had never healed. 'They sent you packing, if I remember correctly.'

Alexa lowered her lashes hastily to veil the pain in her eyes, and the bitter taste of gall was in her mouth as she rose to her feet to lean against the wooden railings surrounding the *stoep*. She stood slim and straight and as rigid as a statue while she absorbed the fragrant silence of her surroundings, and she was somehow rewarded with a strange calmness and an inner strength.

'My uncle and aunt provided me with a home during the school holidays only because they discovered I was willing to earn my keep by taking over some of the chores in the hotel,' she explained without reproach, her eyes staring out across the vast and rugged veld beyond the camp to where the sun was setting like a ball of fire in the west. 'They knew so little about me that I don't really blame them for being so ready to believe everything they were told.'

'How long did it take you to think that one up?'

His ruthless, derisive mockery was laced with that familiar contempt, and it was like a heated blade being thrust into her soul. It plunged her into that dark, hellish hole of despair that brought helpless tears to her eyes, but she blinked them away hastily before she turned slowly to face Revil who was thirstily draining his second can of beer.

'Your mind has become so twisted with the desire for revenge that you wouldn't recognise the truth even if it was staring you in the face.'

Revil was deaf to the bitterness and despair in her voice. His driving need to uncover the truth was like an all-consuming fire inside him, and he had warned her that he would delve painfully deep until he found what he was looking for. A compassionate warmth surged unbidden into her heart, but that did not prevent her from acknowledging that stab of fear at the blazing fury in his eyes when he crushed the can in his hand as if it were made of paper, and rose to his feet like a stealthy jungle cat about to pounce on its prey.

Her nerves vibrated, she felt like a trapped animal, and she stood defenceless when he thrust a hand into the hair at the nape of her neck, his fingers scattering her tortoiseshell combs so that her hair cascaded down in a silvery, silken mass on to her shoulders. He was so close to her that the heat of his body seemed to burn her through her clothes, and she was in mortal fear of her neck snapping when he jerked her head back.

'I have to hand it to you, Alexa,' he snarled savagely down into her upturned face, his glance raking her pale cheeks and soft, quivering lips. 'You have the ability to make me feel like a swine, and at a time like this I annoyingly find myself toying with the idea that my loyalty might perhaps be misplaced.'

She stared up at him helplessly, not knowing what to say in the face of such an astounding confession, and for one fraction of a second it was desire instead of fury she saw burning in his eyes, but he released her almost at once with a muttered oath on his lips and strode into the bungalow in search of Byron Rockford's houseboy who was to show them to their quarters.

Alexa followed Revil and the houseboy in silence along the flagstone path that led towards thatch-roofed bungalows which stood grouped together on the side of the hill overlooking the dam. The mopani and various other indigenous trees were casting long shadows across the well-kept lawns at that late hour of the day, and Alexa could barely wait to be alone in one of those quaint bungalows up ahead of them. She longed for a cool shower and the opportunity to exchange her warm clothes for something cooler, but most of all she longed to be alone for a while.

The houseboy unlocked one of the bungalows, handed the key to Revil, and bowed himself away hastily. Alexa stared after his hastily retreating figure, and brushed aside that uneasy feeling as she preceded Revil into the cool bungalow.

The curtains at the windows matched the colourful, African design of the woven rugs which lay scattered across the tiled floor of the pine-and-cane-furnished living-area, and on one of the woven rugs Revil's weekend bag had been placed neatly beside her own.

A wave of panic swept through Alexa, and she spun round to face Revil. 'There must be some mistake.'

'There has been no mistake,' he smiled twistedly, closing the door and dropping the key with a clatter on to the small table beneath the window. 'We'll be sharing this bungalow during our stay here at Izilwane.'

'But that's out of the question!' she protested, her throat so tight that her voice had been reduced to a husky, frightened croak.

'My dear Alexa, if you'd care to take a look around, you'll find that there are two bedrooms to this bungalow,' Revil mocked her, his hands resting on his lean hips when he surveyed her with a derisive smile curving his sensuous mouth. 'There is, unfortunately, only one bathroom, but I dare say we'll manage.'

'I couldn't care less if this was a thirty-bedroomed mansion with an equal number of bathrooms!' she exploded frantically, backing away towards the door on legs that were beginning to shake like jelly. 'I'm not staying here with you, and when I find your friend, Byron Rockford, I'm going to tell him so!'

Alexa's heart was beating wildly in her throat when she turned her back on Revil's hateful mockery, but she could feel his eyes burning holes into a spot between her shoulder blades. Her mind was intent on escaping. She *could* not, and *would* not stay with him, alone, in that bungalow. She fumbled blindly for the brass door handle, her damp palm slipping on the polished surface as she turned it.

'Please feel free to do as you please,' his mocking laugh stopped her when she had opened the door, 'this happens to be the only vacant bungalow in the game park, but Byron will gladly supply you with a sleeping bag if you prefer to sleep outside with the snakes and the insects.'

'Snakes and insects?' she echoed with a shudder, closing the door abruptly and turning to face Revil who had not moved from the spot where he stood. 'Are there really snakes in this part of the country?'

'If you don't believe me . . .' He smiled, leaving his sentence unfinished as he gestured towards the door, and Alexa could almost hate him for that calm, confident expression on his tanned, handsome features.

She was defeated and he knew it . . . *damn him*! If this was the only vacant bungalow in the game park, then she would have to share it with him. There were, after all, two bedrooms, but that thought was of little comfort to her.

'Are you staying, or are you going?' he demanded

with a hint of growing impatience in his voice, and Alexa resigned herself rather reluctantly to the inevitable.

She faced him with as much dignity as she could muster, and her violet-blue eyes were as cool as her voice. 'I'm staying because you know as well as I do that I can't attempt the alternative.'

'In that case you may use the bathroom first, and be quick about it,' he said abruptly, picking up his bag and striding into one of the bedrooms.

He closed the door firmly behind him, confident that she would not escape him, and a shiver of apprehension raced through her as she lifted her bag off the floor and entered the bedroom which lay in the opposite direction to Revil's.

She felt uncomfortable and wary. Revil could be ruthless and savage, but he could also be kind and gentle, and she was not sure which she feared most. It was a disquieting situation, and it angered her to feel that way.

She zipped open her bag with a savage movement to give vent to some of her feelings, and she took out her sponge bag along with a pair of cotton slacks and a fashionable shirt.

The bathroom led off the living-area, and Alexa locked the door securely behind her before she stripped off her hot, dusty clothes and stepped into the shower cubicle. She opened the cold water tap, and revelled briefly in the icy jet of water against her heated body before she washed her hair and soaped herself. She stepped beneath the spray again, and watched the soapy suds sliding down along her body. Her breasts were too small; it was a fact Alexa had always secretly bewailed, but there had been nothing immature about the way they had reacted to Revil's touch.

Oh, God! she groaned inwardly. Why did she have to

think of that, and why did it have to be Revil Bradstone who had not only touched her body, but her heart in such a way that she now felt bound to him with invisible chains?

'Hurry up! You're not the only one who needs a shower!' Revil's harsh voice intruded on her painful and bewildered thoughts, and she hastily turned off the taps.

'I'll be out in a minute!' she shouted back guiltily.

It took a little more than a minute before she emerged from the bathroom with a small towel wrapped about her head, and dressed in white slacks with a baggy, yellow shirt.

'About time!' Revil bellowed at her in mock anger, and Alexa's pulses jerked violently when she glanced at him.

He was barefoot, just as she was, and he had discarded his black sweater to leave his sun-browned, muscled torso bare. Short, dark hair curled against the skin across his broad chest, and it tapered down his flat, taut-muscled stomach to disappear beneath the belt that hugged his denims to his lean hips.

Alexa's senses were spinning beneath the assault of his raw masculinity. Her heartbeat was erratic, her breath was coming jerkily past her lips, and she was incapable of moving when he walked towards her. She tried to look away only to find her glance trapped by the smoky fire in his eyes, and she was trembling violently when he stood less than a pace away from her.

The towel was whipped off her head, and a steely arm was clamped about her waist, as he pulled her against his hard body. For one brief second his eyes burned down into hers, then his hard mouth claimed hers with a searing, sensual passion that fired the blood racing through her veins. His hands were beneath her yellow shirt, their warmth against the cool, soft skin at her waist arousing dormant nerves to the pleasure of his touch, and she could not suppress the sudden desire to touch him as he was touching her. His kisses were intoxicating, and her hands slid across his shoulders, revelling in their exploration of the rippling muscles beneath his smooth skin before she pushed her fingers into the dark, neatly trimmed hair growing so strongly into his neck.

Dear God, what was it about this man that he could awaken such extraordinary feelings in her?

Revil released her abruptly, and for one frightening second she thought he had guessed her feelings, but, of course, he had not.

'As a sample that wasn't bad,' he murmured, a mocking glint in his eyes. 'It makes me want more, but I guess that will have to wait until later this evening.'

The swift ebb and flow of blood towards the surface of her skin made her embarrassingly aware of the fact that she was blushing profusely. She was not sure whether he was serious, or simply trying to frighten her, but she was not going to wait to find out. She fled to the safety of her bedroom with the sound of his mocking laughter ringing in her ears.

CHAPTER SIX

IT was a warm night, and the silence outside the bungalow was disturbed only by the strange sounds of the bushveld game park. A sound which was more familiar intruded on the silence. It was the sound of Revil's heavy footsteps approaching her bedroom door, and Alexa stiffened on the stool in front of the pine dressing-table, her heartbeat quickening. Her reflection in the mirror told her that she looked calm and poised, her ash-blonde hair shining like pure silk after the vigorous brushing she had given it, but there was a tell-tale tremor in her hand when she put down her brush.

The sharp tap on her door, although expected, made her react with a nervous start, and the door opened before she could utter a sound.

'May I come in?' asked Revil, approaching her where she sat rigidly on the stool in front of the mirror with her heart beating suffocatingly in her throat.

Slacks the colour of rich cream clung to his lean hips and long, muscular legs, and his white, short-sleeved shirt had been left open almost to his waist as if fastening the buttons would make the material stretch too tightly across his wide shoulders and powerful chest. His hair was still damp after his shower and it was brushed back severely from his broad forehead, but his grey eyes still had that strange fire smouldering in their depths. Dear God, did he have to exude such a devastating aura of masculinity, and did her senses have to respond to it so wildly?

'Why bother to ask whether you may come in when

you don't wait for a reply,' she accused, sweeping her hair together in the nape of her neck, and twisting it into its usual coil.

'Leave your hair down.' He stepped behind her, his arresting image trapped with hers in the circular mirror as he gripped her wrists and drew her hands away from her hair to let it cascade down to her shoulders. She could feel her pulses beating fast against his fingers before he released her, and she was almost too afraid to move while she watched him push his fingers through the silken mass of her hair as if it fascinated him to touch it. His eyes met hers unexpectedly in the mirror and he smiled faintly. 'I like it this way.'

'What do you want, Revil?' she asked huskily, passing the tip of her pink tongue nervously along her dry lips, and his glance sharpened on that innocently provocative action.

'I could draw up a long list of what I want, but all the items on it could be chiselled down to one basic need.' He lifted the weight of her hair away from her neck, and his warm mouth against a sensitive spot below her ear sent a thousand little sparks of unwanted pleasure racing along her receptive nerves. 'I want *you*, Alexa,' he murmured into her small, shell-like ear before he straightened, and she shrank from him physically and mentally.

'I'm not an object in a shop window, and you can't have me,' she protested coldly.

'Don't be so sure of that, angel face,' he smiled, amusement lurking in his eyes as he removed his hands from her hair, and thrust them into his pockets while he held her glance in the mirror. 'I have a very strong feeling that I could have you whenever it pleases me.'

'No!'

Her fierce objection evoked a bark of mocking laughter that made her cringe inwardly. 'I used to amuse

...be tempted!

See inside for special
4 FREE BOOKS offer

Harlequin Presents®

Discover deliciously different
romance with 4 Free Novels from

Harlequin Presents

Sit back and enjoy four exciting romances—yours **FREE** from Harlequin Reader Service! But wait . . . there's *even more* to this great offer!

A Useful, Practical Digital Clock/Calendar—FREE

As a free gift simply to thank you for accepting four free books we'll send you a stylish digital quartz clock/calendar—a handsome addition to any decor! The changeable, month-at-a-glance calendar pops out, and may be replaced with a favorite photograph.

PLUS A FREE MYSTERY GIFT—a surprise bonus that will delight you!

All this just for trying our Reader Service!

MONEY-SAVING HOME DELIVERY

Once you receive 4 FREE books and gifts, you'll be able to preview more great romance reading in the convenience of your own home at less than retail prices. Every month we'll deliver 8 brand-new Harlequin Presents novels right to your door months before they appear in stores. If you decide to keep them, they'll be yours for only $2.24 each! That's 26¢ less per book than the retail price—plus 89¢ postage and handling per shipment. And you may cancel at any time, for any reason, and still keep your free books and gifts, just by dropping us a line!

BE TEMPTED! COMPLETE, DETACH AND MAIL YOUR POSTPAID ORDER CARD TODAY AND RECEIVE 4 FREE BOOKS, A DIGITAL CLOCK/CALENDAR AND MYSTERY GIFT—PLUS LOTS MORE!

myself in my childhood by catching butterflies in a net to observe their markings, and they used to flutter about as if I intended imprisoning them for life.'

'And I happen to remind you of a butterfly in a net,' she added distastefully.

'Yes, you do.' A hand emerged from his pocket, and his fingers trailed a lazy, destructive path from her elbow to her smooth shoulder, and down again along her slender throat to slide inside the vee opening of her blouse. 'You want me as much as I want you, but in denying it you're battering your beautiful wings against a net of your own making.'

His sensuous touch against the curve of her breasts was a pleasurable torment, and it aroused a longing which was almost too painful to endure. It was true, she wanted him, but she wanted much more than the physical satisfaction which she was beginning to suspect his body could give her.

'Is this part of the punishment you've planned for me, Revil?' she asked with a hint of sarcasm in her voice when she had succeeded in controlling her feelings.

His disturbing caress ceased abruptly, and his hand once again plunged into his pocket. 'There is pleasure as well as pain in most things that life has to offer.'

'And you intend to have your fill of pleasure at my expense before you inflict pain,' she persisted, and his smoky eyes narrowed to icy slits.

'Pain is something we mostly inflict on ourselves by our thoughtless behaviour, wouldn't you say?'

'That's a debatable point,' she countered swiftly, and his mouth twitched with a semblance of a smile.

'Izilwane is not the ideal place for an argument.' His hands gripped her shoulders lightly, and his mocking glance held hers in the mirror while he lowered his head to press his lips against her hair in a kiss. 'The peace and tranquillity of the bushveld tends to rob me of the desire to be aggressive.'

His image disappeared in the mirror before she could think of an adequate reply, and she drew a jerky breath, turning her head to watch him stride towards the door.

'Take a stroll down to Byron's bungalow when you're ready,' he instructed, pausing when he reached the door and smiling at her over his shoulder in a way that made her bones feel as if they were melting. 'I'll be waiting there for you.'

He closed the door behind him, and Alexa sat as if mesmerised while she listened to his footsteps crossing the living-area of the bungalow. She heard the outer door being opened and closed, and during the ensuing silence she lowered her quivering face into her hands.

'God, help me!' she prayed softly, her voice muffled in her hands. 'I don't have the strength to protect myself against Revil.'

She didn't receive an answer to that prayer, she didn't expect one, and she sat for some time listening to the night sounds before she dabbed a little of her favourite perfume behind her ears and left the bungalow to join Revil.

It was dark outside, but the sky was studded with stars, and the moon was full, lighting the path for her with its silvery glow. She drew the clean, fresh air deep into her lungs, and her step was suddenly light as she walked down to Byron Rockford's bungalow to the accompaniment of noisy crickets in the undergrowth and frogs croaking somewhere far off in a *vlei*.

A fire had been lit. Alexa could smell the wood-smoke in the air, and she could see the glow of it spreading across the lawn as she approached Byron's bungalow.

'There's an old tribal saying in these parts,' she heard Byron remark as she rounded the corner of his bungalow. 'When you dip your arrows in poison, take care not to prick your finger.'

Alexa's curiosity was aroused. What had prompted Byron to make that remark? she wondered amusedly as she walked towards the two men lounging in comfortable cane chairs which had been arranged around a fire burning in a drum which was halved in the length, and placed on a four-legged steel stand. A fire like that could mean only one thing, and her mouth watered at the thought. They were going to have a *braai.* Byron looked up and rose to his feet when he saw Alexa walking towards them.

'Come and join us, Alexa.' Byron forestalled any reply which Revil might have made to his odd remark, and he gestured towards the low table beside his chair. 'May I offer you a glass of wine?'

'Thank you,' Alexa smiled, accepting his offer, and an eerie howl pierced the silence as she lowered herself into the vacant chair beside Revil. 'What's that?' she demanded sharply.

'Jackal,' Byron answered abruptly, placing a glass of white wine in her hand, and she shivered.

'It sounds weird.'

'It's a sound that will give you goose-flesh until you get used to it,' laughed Revil, sliding his hand in a vaguely comforting gesture along her arm, and she was humiliatingly sure he could feel the tiny hairs standing on end against her skin, but he removed his hand almost at once and turned to Byron who had resumed his seat. 'When do you expect the building operations to be completed?'

'I have every hope that it will be completed by the end of this year,' Byron estimated roughly. 'I've put all my available funds into this operation, and I'm fast reaching the stage where I'll need a financial feedback. We also need publicity, and that's where you come in, Revil.'

The fire died down while the men talked and drank their beer, and the steaks and *boerewors* were placed on the grid which Byron had shifted on to the drum. Alexa listened to them talking while they stood around the fire and turned the meat periodically. She loved the sound of Revil's voice, and she loved the way he reasoned and argued the point he was trying to make. Oh, lord, she was falling under his spell like someone falling under a bus. Both could be equally devastating.

The smell of meat grilling on the open fire enhanced her appetite, but her mind was whirling with the many facets of advertising Revil had been discussing with Byron. Her interest was keenly aroused and, during a lull in their discussion, she asked, 'Have you thought of using models in your advertising campaign?'

'Models?' Byron shot the question at Alexa with a blank look on his rugged, deeply tanned features.

Alexa felt Revil's eyes on her, and she was relieved that the darkness hid her blushes at the knowledge that she could have had the audacity to voice her thoughts, and suggest something to a man who knew the advertising world like the palm of his hand. Byron was waiting for an explanation, but it felt as if her tongue had been glued to the roof of her mouth.

'I think what Alexa has in mind,' Revil stepped into the breach, 'is a session with models dressed in fashionable safari outfits, and photographed in a way which would advertise the facilities you will be providing here at Izilwane.'

A wisp of cloud drifted across the moon during the ensuing silence, and a jackal howled again in the distance, sending a shiver up Alexa's spine.

'That's a damn good idea!' Byron finally voiced his opinion. 'What do you think, Revil?'

Revil turned, his eyes glittering strangely in the moonlight, and a faint smile curving his mouth as he studied Alexa intently for a brief, petrifying moment. 'I think that if Alexa ever decided to give up her modelling career I might consider offering her a job on my company's advisory committee.'

Alexa could not be sure whether he was complimenting her or mocking her, but, to be on the safe side, she injected a hint of mockery into her own voice. 'I shall decline your offer, Revil, but thanks anyway.'

'Pity,' he shrugged his wide shoulders, 'you've just put forward a brilliant idea.'

'An idea which, I'm sure, you would have thought of without my assistance,' she conceded, feeling vaguely embarrassed at having drawn attention to herself.

'I hate to be the one to break up this newly formed mutual admiration society,' Byron interrupted humorously, 'but the meat is done.'

Byron's houseboy had brought out salads and bread rolls while the meat had been *braaiing*, and he had set it out on a slatted table with all the necessary cutlery and crockery. They helped themselves to the tender steaks and spicy *boerewors*, and filled their plates with the attractively prepared salads. Alexa lapsed into silence while they ate, listening to Revil and Byron discussing Byron's expectations for the game park. The now familiar howl of a jackal could again be heard in the distance, but this time it didn't affect Alexa as it had in the beginning. She was in a strange environment, but the peace and tranquillity Revil had mentioned seemed to wash away the fears and anxiety which had made her so incredibly tense earlier.

The atmosphere was relaxed around the drum where the glowing embers of the fire were dying down swiftly. Revil joked and laughed as Byron related amusing incidents which had occurred during his career as a game ranger, and Alexa couldn't help thinking that Revil needed to laugh more often. Laughter softened his stern features; it also gave her yet another glimpse of the *real* man behind that harsh, often mocking mask he presented to her, and a longing stirred deep down inside her which she knew had to be quelled at all costs.

She was having difficulty in keeping her eyes open, and she could not decide whether to blame it on the two glasses of wine or the good food she had consumed. Revil and Byron's voices seemed to drift continually into the distance, and her head actually bobbed once with fatigue.

'Forgive me,' she apologised eventually, stifling a yawn behind her fingers, and rising to her feet. 'I don't mean to be rude, but I simply can't stay awake a minute longer.'

'You're excused, Alexa, if you want to go to bed,' Revil announced from the depths of his chair, making her feel like a child, but Byron rose politely, giving her some recognition, at least, as an adult.

'Goodnight, Alexa,' he said gravely, 'and a word of warning. I might not have lions roaming about the park, but some of the animals are potentially dangerous, and I wouldn't advise you to wander beyond the gates of the camp at any time during the weekend without an escort.'

'No need to worry,' she assured him sincerely. 'Much as I'd love to see the animals in your game park, I have no intention of venturing out on my own.'

She said goodnight and left, finding her way back to the bungalow in the moonlit darkness. She was exhausted, and she washed quickly and brushed her teeth before going to bed. Unaccustomed to the silence, she lay for a while staring into the darkness, but her eyelids felt heavy, and she was asleep within seconds.

Her dreams were distorted and filled with varying images of Revil. She had vivid images of Revil looking furious, and then smiling; subjecting her to the savageness of his contempt, and then treating her with an infinite tenderness. The complexity of her dream was disturbing, and yet she didn't want it to end. He was seated beside her on the bed, leaning over her, and gently stroking her hair away from her face. His light, almost tender touch awakened feelings that rose like a fountain inside her, and she sighed contentedly, a smile on her lips as she turned her cheek into the warm palm of his hand.

It took but a fraction of a startled second to discover that this was no longer a dream; this was a reality, and her sharp, indrawn breath was a loud hiss in the silence. The door stood open, and the light from the living-area shone into her bedroom. Revil was seated beside her on the bed, and he was, in reality, leaning over her and stroking her cheek with his fingers.

His face was partly in shadow, and her heart thudded against her ribs when she realised that he wasn't wearing a shirt. She didn't question his presence, and for some obscure reason she no longer feared what she had begun to consider as inevitable. If she was going to lose her virginity, then she was strangely relieved that it was Revil who would be robbing her of it.

'I never intended waking you, but you're so beautiful, Alexa, I can't seem to keep my hands off you,' he whispered, lowering his head, and blotting out the shaft of light that shone into her bedroom.

His mouth brushed lightly against hers, the tip of his moist tongue trailing along the outline of her lips and teasing the corners of her mouth until her lips parted in eager anticipation of the kiss she longed for. His hard mouth shifted over hers at last, his tongue invading the sweetness within, and her trembling hands began their eager exploration of the muscled hardness of his shoulders before her fingers lingered in a caress at the nape of his neck.

This had to be part of a beautiful dream, her drugged mind decided, when Revil's fingers tugged at the narrow satin bow and parted the frothy lace at the bodice of her nightgown to gain access to her breasts. His sensual touch aroused emotions which frightened as well as excited her, and her gasp of pleasure ended in a whimper of ecstasy when his mouth left hers in search of the tender, rounded flesh which had swelled beneath his probing, stroking fingers. His tongue flicked repeatedly across the hardened peak of her breast in an erotic caress before his warm, moist mouth closed over it, and the languid warmth flowing through her body was suddenly accompanied by a sweet, sharp stab of desire in her loins that made her arch her hips towards his in an invitation which had been motivated by instinct rather than by knowledge.

'God, Alexa, but I want you,' he murmured throatily, flinging back the sheets, and lying down beside her on the double bed.

Alexa could not answer him, her heart was beating too fast to speak, and those strong hands on her sensitised body were creating delightful havoc with her emotions. His hand was sliding beneath her nightgown, stroking her shapely thighs, the curve of her hips to her waist, and down again across her flat stomach, but a breath of sanity invaded her drugged mind when his hand ventured lower. She could not be sure whether she had withdrawn physically, or whether Revil had merely sensed her inner withdrawal, but his mouth closed over hers swiftly, stifling whatever protest she might have made and, forcing her thighs apart with his knee, his gentle, stroking fingers invaded the most intimate part of her body.

The sensations surging through her awakened every nerve and sinew to a level of physical pleasure she had never encountered before, and any thought of resistance which she might have nurtured was buried beneath that wild and primitive desire which was pulsating through her. No one had ever touched her like this before, and no one, other than Revil, ever would again. His touch was sufficient to make her belong to him, mind, body and soul, and she did not want it any other way.

Passion was a fire that made the blood flow through her veins like volcanic lava, and it consumed her until her mind was totally devoid of coherent thought. She was unaware of what she was doing; she was conscious only of the clean, male smell of Revil, and the feel of taut, quivering muscles beneath his damp skin while his hot mouth ravaged hers. She was aware also of an aching need to get closer to him, to have his aroused body filling that throbbing void inside her, but, with an abruptness that left her stunned, he thrust himself away from her and sat up.

She could hear a drum beating out a pagan rhythm, and for one crazy moment she imagined they were somewhere in the heart of a jungle, but she was mistaken. She had been listening to the beat of her own heart, and it was beating out a troubled, anxious message. What was wrong?

'Revil?' She tried to read the expression in his eyes when he turned his head to look at her, but his face was in shadow.

'Not yet, Alexa,' he said tersely, getting up and walking towards the door. 'Some other time, but not yet.'

It took a moment for her hazy mind to recognise that note of harsh mockery in his voice, and she went hot, then cold when she realised what he had said.

'Damn you, Revil!' she said with an anger born of shame and humiliation as she sat up in bed and dragged the sheets about her partially naked, quivering body. 'Do you have to say that, and make it sound as if I was going to ask you to make love to me?'

He paused in the doorway, the light shining full on his harsh, mocking features, and he raised one dark, sardonic eyebrow. 'Weren't you?'

'No!' she almost screamed at him, but deep down inside there was a little voice that cried out the opposite.

'In time to come you will, you know,' he taunted her.

'Never!'

'It will give me great pleasure to prove you a liar.' His soft, derisive laughter made the blood surge into her face and recede again to leave her pale and wide-eyed. 'It will be the easiest thing on earth to make you beg me to make love to you, and then I shall remind you of what you said this evening.'

'I'd rather die than allow you that victory!' she told him fiercely, but in her heart she knew exactly how little difficulty he would have in obtaining it, and, worst of all, Revil knew it too.

'Sleep well, Alexa,' he smiled mockingly, leaving her room and closing the door behind him.

Alexa squirmed inwardly with shame and mortification at the memory of the intimacies she had allowed, and this was the moment her mind chose to remind her of Carol Ross's warning. *Don't fall in love with this man!* 'Oh, God, it's too late!' she groaned in anguish, burying her hot face in the sheet she was still clutching against her trembling body. 'I've committed that unforgivable crime. I have fallen in love with Revil, and I shall have to spend the rest of my life paying for it!'

Alexa awoke the following morning to the sound of loud banging on the outer door of the bungalow. Her hand reached out for her watch on the bedside cupboard and she squinted at it. Seven-thirty! Good heavens! She had had less than three hours' sleep. The banging was resumed, and she groaned, clutching her throbbing head as she dragged herself out of bed and pulled on her robe to stagger from her room.

Her eyes protested violently to the bright, early morning sunshine, and she had to blink several times before she recognised Byron's houseboy standing on the doorstep. He thrust a tray at her which was covered with a white cloth, and he disappeared almost before she could thank him.

Where was Revil? She kicked the door shut with her foot, and the stab of pain that shot through her head when the door banged made her wince when she placed the tray on the low table beside a chair. One glance through the open door into Revil's bedroom told her that he was not there, and she sighed with relief as she lowered herself weakly on to the chair.

She sat for several seconds staring blankly at the tray before she lifted the cover to find that Byron's houseboy had brought her two boiled eggs, fresh rolls, and a pot of aromatic coffee, and quite suddenly she was hungry.

'Hello, what's this I wonder?' she murmured to herself, a frown creasing her smooth brow when she saw a folded sheet of paper propped up between the sugar bowl and the milk jug, and her heart leapt into her throat when she opened it to find Revil's bold handwriting leaping out at her from the paper.

When you've had your breakfast I suggest you take a walk past Byron's bungalow to the main building. Ask anyone for directions to Byron's office. I'll be waiting there, and be quick about it if you would like to take a drive through the park. Revil.

Alexa crumpled the note in her hand and flung it across the room in a display of temper which was totally alien to her nature. Yesterday the thought of a drive through the park with Revil would have excited her, but not this morning, and not after what had happened last night. She wished that she could refuse to go with him, but she really had no choice. Her refusal would invite further curiosity, and she could not bear that.

She had lost her appetite, but the coffee smelled good, and she poured herself a cup. She drank it quickly before taking a shower and changing into cool beige slacks and a sleeveless blue T-shirt. It was going to be a hot day, she could already feel that oppressive heat attempting to invade the cool bungalow, and she tied her hair back with a matching blue scarf before she applied a light touch of make-up.

During the short walk towards the main building Alexa could see a dozen or more bungalows which were still in the process of being built along the ridge of the hill, and they all overlooked the dam in the distance. The main building itself was not yet completed. The dining-area was being enlarged, a lounge and games room was being added, and it appeared as if provision was being made for two shops.

Byron's office was not difficult to find. It was situated in the original section of the main building and, drawn by the sound of Byron and Revil's voices, she walked towards the door which stood slightly ajar. They were studying something on Byron's paper-strewn desk when she entered, and Byron looked up at the sound of her step on the tiled floor.

'Good morning, Alexa.' He smiled at her briefly. 'Take a seat; we won't be long.'

Revil turned, his blue denims, checked shirt and denim waistcoat accentuating his wide-shouldered, lean-hipped frame. His smoky glance sought hers, but she avoided it skilfully, afraid of the mockery and possibly the contempt she might see there.

'Did you sleep well, Alexa?' Revil questioned her, the sensual warmth in his voice making her cheeks sting with embarrassment, and Alexa wished that the tiled floor would open up beneath her when she saw Byron observing them closely with an odd expression in his tawny eyes.

'I slept very well, thank you,' she lied, her voice clipped with the effort to regain her composure.

Byron drew Revil's attention back to the subject they were discussing when Alexa had arrived, and it afforded her a certain amount of relief to wander around Byron's light, airy office, looking at the framed photographs of various animals hanging against the wall.

On a shelf, almost hidden behind a pile of books, she found six unframed watercolour paintings propped up against the wall, and she removed them carefully. The paintings were all of animals, and the artist's sensitivity and brush technique had succeeded in making them look so alive that Alexa had the oddest feeling they could walk out of the paper at any minute. There was a painting of a kudu, a wildebeest and a gemsbuck, and three other species of buck which she could not identify. She was lowering her glance to the bottom of the paintings, searching for the artist's name, when she became aware of the silence in the office, and she turned with a guilty start, the paintings still clutched in her hands.

'Forgive me for prying, Byron, but I think these paintings are absolutely beautiful,' Alexa apologised. 'Who's the artist?'

'Megan O'Brien from Louisville,' Byron enlightened her with a faintly amused smile curving his strongly chiselled mouth. 'She's a very talented young lady, and she will be leasing one of the shops in this complex to sell her paintings, along with curios and other hand-crafted articles.'

Revil stepped up behind Alexa to study one of the paintings over her shoulder, and he was standing so close to her that she could feel the heat of his body against her back. The faint smell of his masculine cologne stirred her senses, and her nerves started to quiver in response to his nearness, making her recall the intimacies she had allowed the night before which would never cease to make her cringe with shame and humiliation.

'This is just what we need, Byron.' Revil's arm brushed against hers when he took the paintings from her, and that brief touch ignited a thousand sparks as if she had been wired to an electrical current, but he was oblivious of her reaction. 'Do you think this young lady would be interested in doing a couple more for us?' he asked as he spread the paintings out on Byron's desk to study them intently.

'For a fee, I presume?'

'Naturally,' Revil confirmed abruptly without looking up from the paintings, and Byron raised his massive shoulders in a slight shrug.

'I doubt if Megan would refuse,' Byron voiced his opinion, 'but I naturally can't guarantee anything.'

'Set up a meeting for me, Byron, and leave me to do the rest.' Revil's features radiated confidence and determination, and Alexa could almost predict the outcome of a meeting between Revil and the artist of those exquisite paintings. 'Come on, Alexa,' Revil interrupted her thoughts. 'We've got Byron's Land Rover for the morning, and if we don't leave now we won't be back in time for lunch.'

He gripped her arm, ushering her out of the office and

out of the building to where Byron's green Land Rover was parked in the shade of the acacia trees. The sun was stinging her skin, and she didn't hesitate to get into the vehicle. Her skin was so pale that she very easily burnt herself into an uncomfortable state, and she had not thought to bring a protective lotion with her when she had packed her bag in such a hurry the day before.

Revil slid in behind the wheel, and the Land Rover's powerful engine roared to life when he turned the key in the ignition. Alexa sat stiffly beside him, aware of him with every fibre of her being, and aware too of the way he looked at her from time to time as he drove along the road that wound its way amongst the bungalows towards the gates at the entrance to the camp.

'You look a bit peaky this morning,' he mocked her when they had passed through the gate and were driving slowly along the graded road through the park. 'I wonder why?'

Alexa felt a stab of anger so intense that she had to clench her hands in her lap to quell the desire to strike him. 'If that's supposed to be funny, then I can assure you it isn't.'

'Don't you find it amusing that I could want you when I ought to feel nothing but contempt for you?' His features were distorted with a savage anger when he glanced at her briefly and added through his teeth, 'God knows, I find it hilarious, and I despise myself for it!'

Alexa bit down hard on her quivering lip to ease the pain he had inflicted. He was hurting her, but, for some strange reason, she suspected that he was hurting himself as well. It was crazy, but she could not shake off that feeling.

'Have you got nothing to say to that?' he barked at her when she remained silent.

'What would you want me to say, Revil?' she asked

bitterly. 'You made it quite clear at our first meeting in your office that you felt nothing but contempt for me. I can, however, understand how you must despise yourself for wanting me, and all I can offer you is my sympathy, but that isn't what you want. Is it?'

'No, *damn* you, I don't want your sympathy!' he exploded, stepping hard on the brakes, and bringing the Land Rover to a skidding halt beneath an acacia tree to send a troupe of baboons scattering in several directions with loud, indignant barks. He turned towards her with a savage movement, and she was trapped by the angry fire in his smoky eyes. 'You wanted me last night as much as I wanted you, didn't you?'

Yes, she had wanted him. She had wanted him so much that she had been ready to place herself on the altar of her love for him in order to prove her innocence, if nothing else. But she couldn't say that. She could *never* say that!

'You don't need confirmation of that, Revil. You're an experienced lover, you know how to arouse a woman, and I didn't really stand a chance.' She hid her pain successfully behind her cool, direct gaze. 'Does that satisfy you?'

He smiled twistedly. 'For the moment, yes.'

CHAPTER SEVEN

A WAVE of helplessness surged through Alexa as she sat staring at Revil, and a hidden part of her wanted to join in the chorus when the cicadas started shrieking loudly in the trees.

'I think I know what your goal is, Revil,' she broke the silence between them, her soft voice tainted with bitterness. 'It's not so much my body you're aiming at, it's my mind and my soul you want to possess. You want to awaken a need in me which only you can assuage; you want to enslave me completely until I'm begging like a starved dog for the crumbs you might care to toss my way, and then you want to see me writhing in mental and physical anguish at your feet while you stand up there on your lofty, self-righteous pedestal and reject me. Oh, but that isn't all you have planned for me,' she smiled with unaccustomed cynicism. 'The mental and physical agony I shall suffer won't be enough to satisfy your desire for revenge. You've got to have more, *much* more, and you're in the right position to accomplish whatever you set out to do. A word here and there in the right direction could ruin my career, and no one wields more power in the advertising world than you do. That's your true goal, isn't it, Revil?'

He had gone strangely white about the mouth as if her angry resumé had shocked and insulted him, but that hard glitter of mockery still lingered in his eyes.

'That was quite a speech, my dear,' he applauded her with a derisive smile, 'I hope you feel better now that you've got all that off your chest?'

She felt choked. How much longer could she bear his mockery and his insults? She stared out of the window beside her, but tears blurred her vision, and she was desperately trying to blink them away when Revil's fingers gripped her chin to force her head round until he saw the glimmer of moisture in her eyes which she had tried to hide.

'Tears, Alexa?' he continued to mock her ruthlessly. 'If you think that resorting to tears will solve the problem, then you're mistaken, my dear, so you might as well dry them, and accept the fact that I'm going to be as harsh on you as I am on myself until I know every intimate detail about you.'

'I hate you, Revil Bradstone!' she hissed, slapping his hand away and searching without success for a handkerchief only to have to endure the added humiliation of having to accept the one she was offered.

'Take care, darling,' he warned, pocketing his handkerchief when she had completed the mopping up process, and turning the key in the Land Rover's ignition. 'They say hate is akin to love and, if that's true, I might have you loving me as well as wanting me.'

A cloud of dust billowed out behind the Land Rover when he pulled away, and Alexa sat for a long time without speaking, trying to overcome her misery and regain her composure. *Hate is akin to love*; Revil's words echoed repeatedly through her mind. Yes, she could see the truth in that. Only someone you loved could hurt and insult you sufficiently to make you hate them. If she hadn't been foolish enough to fall in love with Revil, then he would not have had the power to hurt her so much. Oh, *damn*! Why did it have to be Revil Bradstone, of all people!

Revil had been driving slowly for the past half-hour, but she glanced at him sharply when he brought the

Land Rover to a careful halt at the side of the road without switching off the engine.

'Why are we stopping?' she asked nervously.

'I want to show you something you might not be lucky enough to see again,' he smiled, his arm sliding about her shoulders. 'Lean this way, and let your eyes follow the direction I'm pointing.'

Curiosity prompted her to do as she was told, and Revil's hands were on her shoulders, drawing her towards him until she was leaning with her back against his broad chest. It was disturbing to feel the heat of his body against her own, but she tried to ignore the sensations spiralling through her while she stared in the direction he was pointing.

In amongst the trees, almost hidden by the foliage, stood a magnificent animal with corkscrew horns, and Alexa felt her heartbeat quicken at the sight of it.

'It's a kudu, isn't it?' she whispered, almost too afraid to speak, and totally enthralled.

'Yes,' Revil murmured close to her ear, his breath stirring the hair against her temple. 'The kudu is generally a shy and elusive creature, and its striped grey coat often acts as a perfect camouflage in the bush.'

The kudu bull stood absolutely still, and there was not a detectable quiver in its massive, muscled body. If it was aware of their presence, then it gave no sign, and Alexa found herself incapable of dragging her eyes away from something which she had seen only in photographs before.

'It's beautiful and . . . oh, it's gone!' she sighed ruefully when the swaying of a low-hanging branch was the only indication that the kudu had been there.

Her attention suddenly became focused on something more dangerous than the kudu. She was aware of Revil's hands lingering on her shoulders, and the quickening pace of his heart thudding into her back. Her own heart was beginning to race, and the tightening of his fingers against her slim shoulders warned her of the danger in prolonging this physical contact between them. She drew away from him, escaping his touch, and she rigidly avoided looking at him when he drove on through the park, but it took a while before her pulse slowed down to its normal pace.

It was hot in the Land Rover even though the windows were open. The cicadas were shrilling loudly, not a breeze stirred the leaves on the trees, and she could feel her T-shirt clinging rather uncomfortably to her back. The heat and the drone of the Land Rover's engine was making her drowsy, but she was wide awake when they entered a large clearing amongst the trees.

'Oh, look!' Alexa exclaimed softly, pointing towards several species of buck grazing in the veld, and Revil stopped the Land Rover beneath a shady acacia tree.

'This appears to be your lucky day,' he smiled at her without his usual mockery as he switched off the Land Rover's engine, and her heart turned over in her breast.

If only he would smile at her like that more often. If only . . .! She tugged sharply at the reins of her mind. At that precise moment it would be much safer to concentrate on focusing her attention on the animals.

The blue wildebeest was not difficult to recognise with its long-faced, buffalo-like head, and then there was the sleeker-looking gemsbuck with its long, rapier-like horns, and the defining black stripe extending along the lower sides of its greyish brown body. She had read somewhere that a gemsbuck had been known to kill a lion by impaling it on its horns, but she had no idea how true this was, and they looked so docile grazing in amongst the wildebeest and impala that she could not attribute such ferocity to them.

'They look so calm and contented, and it seems a pity that Byron is going to introduce lion into the park to shatter the peaceful existence of those animals.' She voiced her disturbing thoughts with a sadness in her eyes.

'To keep these game animals in manageable proportions one would have to resort to culling them periodically, and that is never a very pleasant task, but with lion in the park culling shouldn't be necessary,' Revil explained, studying her intently. 'Which method would you prefer?'

'Both sound equally drastic,' she laughed self-consciously, 'but I admit that, with lion in the park, Byron would be dealing with the situation in a natural way, and . . .' she shuddered, 'one must not overlook the fact that it would be a tourist attraction.'

Revil was staring at her oddly and so intently that her pulse rate quickened to an alarming pace. 'It seems you're not quite the heartless tramp I believed you to be.'

There was a hint of mockery in his voice, but she was not quite sure whether it was directed at her, or himself. His stare was prolonged, his grey, smoky eyes darkening with an unfathomable emotion which sent little shivers of awareness racing through her, and she was incapable of moving when he leaned towards her to slide his arm along her shoulders.

'You're trembling,' he said, drawing her towards him until she was resting against his chest, and it would have been the most natural thing on earth to lower her head on to his shoulder, but she dared not succumb to that longing.

'Shouldn't we be returning to the camp?' She desperately tried to steer his attention on to safer ground while she tried to free herself, but she found herself trapped suddenly in the circle of his hard arms. 'Let me go, Revil!' she pleaded anxiously.

'I can't,' he muttered throatily, his eyes burning down into hers with that smoky fire of desire that made her breath catch in her throat. 'Dammit, Alexa, I can't seem to keep my hands off you!'

'Revil——'

'Don't say anything!' he stopped her with his fingers against her quivering lips, and there was an oddly tortured expression on his handsome face that wrenched sharply at her heart. 'Don't say anything at all!'

His fingers left her lips to trace her perfectly arched eyebrows, and her eyelids fluttered down beneath his light touch before his fingers trailed across her cheek and down along her throat to where that tell-tale pulse was beating so erratically. She knew he was going to kiss her and, despite everything that had gone before, she longed for it. She felt his breath against her eager, parted lips, and a jerky little sigh escaped her when his warm mouth closed over hers with a passionate intensity that made her senses whirl. It was madness to surrender so easily to a man whose sole aim she believed was to hurt her, but it was a sweet madness that affected her like someone addicted to a drug.

Their lips clung, their hands seeking and finding pleasure in touching each other, and when at last they drew apart they were both breathless and shaken by the intensity of the emotions they had aroused in each other.

Something had happened; something which she could not put a name to, but she could feel it. It was there in the pregnant silence between them as they sat staring at each other, but it was gone the next instant when she saw that familiar flash of anger in Revil's eyes.

'My God, you're——'

'*No!*' This time it was Alexa's fingers that stilled the words on Revil's lips, and she shook her head slowly, a plea in her beautiful eyes. 'Don't spoil this moment,' she warned softly. 'There might never again be anything good between us, but we will at least have this moment to remember.'

The anger was still burning fiercely in his eyes when his hand gripped her wrist, and she thought for one agonising moment that he intended flinging her hand aside in disgust, but he turned his mouth into her palm in a brief, almost savage caress before he released her.

For some obscure reason she wanted to cry, but the thought of his mockery made her choke back her tears. She stared straight ahead of her when he turned the key in the ignition, and they drove back to the camp in silence.

'You have an appointment with Megan O'Brien at two-thirty this afternoon,' Byron informed Revil shortly after they arrived back at the camp.

'Where?' Revil asked in his usual abrupt manner.

'At her home in Louisville, and that's about a twenty-minute drive from here.' Byron turned from Revil to direct his tawny gaze at Alexa. 'You're welcome to come with us, and I can promise you that you'll find her other works of art equally interesting.'

'I'd love to go with you,' Alexa smiled up at him, 'and thank you for inviting me.'

Megan O'Brien's studio was a thatched cottage in the grounds of her parents' home, and all the rooms, excepting the bathroom and kitchen, were crammed with framed paintings, sculptures, clay pots, wood carvings and colourful beadwork. The artist herself was small and slender, and not much older than nineteen. Honey-gold hair curled softly about her small oval face, and a smile seemed to lurk permanently in her blue eyes. She had welcomed them warmly, and with an almost child-like enthusiasm, but beneath that exterior she was adult and professional.

'My studio is rather overcrowded at the moment, but I've started collecting stock for the curio shop at Izilwane,' Megan O'Brien explained apologetically when Revil had successfully concluded their business discussion, and she directed her eager gaze at the khaki-clad man who sat sprawled in one of her floral, comfortably padded armchairs. 'Are you making good progress with the building operations, Byron?'

'The main building ought to be completed within the next two months,' he enlightened her.

'Oh, I can't wait!' she exclaimed excitedly, and her child-like enthusiasm was once again in evidence when she took them on an impromptu tour of the spacious rooms to see her work.

'You surely didn't make all these?' Revil questioned her keenly, his hand making a sweeping gesture to include the African heads carved in wood, the clay pots, and beadwork.

'Good heavens, no!' Megan O'Brien laughed merrily. 'I paint and sculpt a little, but I have a group of artistic native men and women helping me, and the curio shop will be an ideal outlet for their work which, I feel, has that distinct African flavour tourists always find so appealing.'

'And the tapestries?' Alexa intervened quietly, standing back slightly to admire the expertly stitched, framed tapestries propped up against the wall.

'I painted the animals on to the tapestry cloth, and my mother and my aunt did the rest,' Megan smiled.

They were returning to the main part of the air-conditioned cottage when a white Maltese poodle scampered excitedly into the room. It growled at Revil and Byron, took one look at Alexa through its fringe of white hair, and bounded up to her, tail wagging and panting to be picked up.

Alexa did not need a second invitation. She scooped the woolly little thing up into her arms, and she laughed softly, unaware of Revil's eyes regarding her intently while she tried to avoid being licked profusely.

'You are receiving an honour of the highest order, Miss Drew,' said Megan O'Brien, a look of almost stunned surprise on her face. 'Pickles will never go anywhere near strangers, let alone allow them to touch her, so you must be someone special for her to shower you with such effusive attention.'

'I once had a little dog like this.' Alexa lowered Pickles to the floor, and tried to explain away what had suddenly become an embarrassing situation, but she was oblivious of the wistful expression lingering in her eyes. 'When my parents died I had to give my dog away, and it nearly broke my heart to part with her,' she added.

During the ensuing silence Alexa was uncomfortably aware of three pairs of eyes focused on her with varying expressions in their depths, and she could feel the pinkness of embarrassment staining her cheeks when Revil turned to study the pencil sketches of a dark-haired little boy and girl which lay open on a table.

'Did you do these pencil sketches?' he asked Megan O'Brien.

'Yes, Mr Bradstone,' Megan nodded, and her honey-gold curls bobbed about her head as she smiled up at him a little shyly. 'I sketch portraits for relaxation, and the family are always eager to sit for me.'

'I can understand their eagerness,' Revil compliment-ed her. 'These sketches are very good.'

Her shy smile deepened. 'Thank you.'

'How long does it take you to do a sketch like this?'

'Fifteen minutes,' she answered thoughtfully. 'Perhaps

twenty, but it varies from subject to subject.'

'Would you do one of Alexa while I take another look around?'

'I'd be delighted to,' Megan agreed to Revil's request, the sound of her voice drowning out Alexa's gasp of dismay.

'You're not serious, Revil,' Alexa protested hastily, and the atmosphere between them was tense and strained while her mind began a frantic search for one good reason why Revil should want Megan to do a pencil sketch of her.

'I most certainly am serious,' he contradicted her with an unfathomable expression in his smoky eyes before he directed his gaze beyond her. 'Coming with me, Byron?'

Byron excused himself, and then Alexa found herself alone in the room with Megan O'Brien who was setting up her sketch pad on an easel.

Alexa's mind continued to whirl in those frantic, questioning circles. What was the reason behind Revil's request? Why this sudden desire to have Megan O'Brien do a pencil sketch of her? How could he use it against her?

'Would you sit here, Miss Drew?' Megan interrupted Alexa's troubled thoughts, and Alexa lowered herself gingerly on to the stool which Megan had positioned close to the window where the light was good. 'Turn your head a little to your right.'

'Like this?' asked Alexa, obliging the young artist.

'Perfect,' Megan smiled, picking up her pencil. 'Now, all you have to do is relax and forget that I'm here.'

Her smile was infectious, and the corners of Alexa's mouth lifted in an answering smile. 'I'll try.'

Alexa's mind wandered freely while Megan's pencil moved with quick, firm strokes across the paper. Pickles lay stretched out on the floor near Megan's feet, content and happy to be near her mistress, and Alexa could not decide whom she envied the most. Pickles had Megan, and Megan was obviously a member of a happy and very united family. Alexa had no one, and in recent years she had felt that she belonged nowhere and never would. She had a fulfilling job, a job for which she owed Madame Véronique a debt of gratitude which she could never repay entirely, but that was all she had. She did not pity herself; pity was a destructive emotion, but there were times, such as now, when she had difficulty in suppressing that deep-seated longing inside her.

Megan put down her pencil twenty minutes later, tore the page out of her sketch pad, and handed it to Alexa. 'I think you'll find it's a very good likeness.'

It was much more than that, Alexa discovered when she found herself staring at the face she encountered whenever she looked in the mirror. Megan had done much more than simply capture Alexa's features on paper. She had sketched into the generous mouth a tender promise of a passion yet to come, and a warmth and sensitivity which was enhanced by an underlying hint of humour. There was pride in the tilt of her head, but Alexa felt a ripple of shock course through her when she stared into the eyes which were gazing back at her so steadily. Megan O'Brien, young as she was, had looked beyond the mask Alexa showed to the world, and, in doing so, she had bared Alexa's soul on paper. There was warmth and compassion, and that trusting innocence which had plunged her once into the darkest well of misery. Worst of all, there was that suggestion of a great capacity for love which Alexa herself was only just beginning to discover. There was a sadness, too, in the eyes that stared back at her, and a wistful longing.

It was shattering to see herself like this. It felt as if she had been dealt a savage blow that had robbed her of the air in her lungs, and she wondered if Revil had purposely subjected her to this ordeal knowing that Megan O'Brien had the ability to strip her down to her soul. *Damn him! Damn him into hell!*

Alexa stiffened at the sound of footsteps entering the room, and she rose abruptly from the stool, her face a shade whiter than usual. Her nervous glance locked with Revil's, and he held out his hand without speaking for the sketch she still clutched between her trembling fingers. She wished that she could destroy it, but fear of the consequences made her hand it to him so that both he and Byron could look at it.

She studied Revil's expression for some sign of what he might be thinking, but his features remained inscrutable.

'This is excellent work, Megan,' Byron praised the young girl lavishly. 'I'd say she has captured Alexa exactly as she is. Wouldn't you say so, Revil?'

The two men exchanged glances, and something passed between them that set Alexa's nerves on edge. Revil's face became shuttered, and Alexa could almost pick up the vibrations of anger emanating from him, but there was no hint of it in the smile he bestowed upon Megan the next instant.

'How much do I owe you, Miss O'Brien?'

'Nothing, Mr Bradstone,' Megan assured him. 'You've made me such a fantastic offer that I would like you to consider this as a gift.'

'Thank you.' Revil inclined his dark head, his stern features relaxing a fraction. 'Besides being talented, you're also a very generous and gracious young lady.'

Megan blushed becomingly and changed the subject. 'My mother will have tea waiting for us. I hope you're not in a hurry to leave?'

'We'd be delighted to stay for tea,' Revil announced,

placing the sketch in his briefcase, 'but I'm afraid it depends on Byron.'

'There's no rush.' Byron smiled down into Megan's anxious face. 'As long as we're back at Izilwane by five this afternoon.'

'Oh, good!' Megan exclaimed, leading the way out and along a flagstone path through a colourful, well-kept garden towards a two-storeyed house, with Pickles hard on her heels and the rest of them following.

Vivien O'Brien awaited them in her spacious living-room with its attractive mixture of modern and antique furnishings, and her warm hospitality soon banished whatever tensions there might have been in the atmosphere. She was a woman with striking features, dark eyes, and a smattering of grey at the temples of her dark hair which was combed back into an attractive but casual chignon. She was tall and elegant in a cool, floral silk outfit, and she was still remarkably slender for a woman whom Alexa guessed to be somewhere in her early forties.

They were served tea and freshly baked scones, and it was at this point that Pickles decided to turn traitor again. She leapt on to Alexa's lap, curled herself into a ball, and promptly went to sleep, but her action drew Vivien O'Brien's somewhat startled glance to Alexa.

'What do you do for a living, my dear?' she questioned Alexa.

'I'm a model.'

'I should have known,' the older woman smiled, her interested glance lingering on Alexa's slender body. 'You have all the right proportions for someone in that profession. But, tell me, is it always as glamorous as it appears to be, or is there a lot of slogging going on in the background which the public never gets to hear about?'

'There's a lot of training and hard work involved,' Alexa admitted.

'And you, Mr Bradstone? You're the chairman of Bradstone Promotions, are you not?' A look of surprise flashed across Revil's face, and Vivien O'Brien's dark eyes sparkled with humour. 'We may live in a *dorp* far from the big city, but we do read the newspapers and watch television, you know.'

A rueful smile curved Revil's mouth. 'I believe I deserved that rap over the knuckles.'

'It was unintentional,' Vivien O'Brien laughingly assured him, then her expression sobered. 'Megan never mentioned who she had an appointment with this afternoon, and now that I know who you are I have to admit that my womanly curiosity is very much aroused. May I know what this meeting was all about?'

'My company has the contract to promote Byron's game park to the public,' Revil obligingly enlightened her, 'and I've commissioned your daughter to do several watercolour paintings which will be used for advertising purposes.'

'I've always thought that Megan's work is of a high quality, but she has considered my opinion to be slightly biased.' There was a tender warmth in Vivien O'Brien's dark eyes when she smiled at her daughter. 'Perhaps now you will believe me, darling.'

'Oh, Mother!' Megan laughed self-consciously. 'I've always valued your opinion because I've known it was honest, but I doubt if any artist is ever entirely satisfied with their work.

'Aiming at one's own idea of perfection and always finding it just beyond one's reach is a great incentive,' Alexa supported Megan O'Brien's claim, and Megan turned to her eagerly.

'You've found that as well in your profession?'

'I have,' Alexa admitted, 'but I think in any field of work there has to be an incentive to do better if one wants to reach the top.'

'What are you aiming at, Alexa?' Revil intervened, his mockery cleverly disguised by a look of interest. 'The *Model of the Year* award?'

Alexa caught a look in Byron Rockford's eyes which puzzled her. Was it pity, or was it anger? And who was it directed at?

'My aspirations aren't that high,' she answered Revil with a calmness that hid the pain and despair in her heart. 'I simply want to be good at what I'm doing.'

'And happy at it, surely?' Vivien O'Brien intervened calmly, and seemingly unaware of the tension which had leapt unavoidably into the air between Revil and Alexa.

'Happiness, like everything else, never comes easily,' Alexa said, while trying desperately to ignore that hint of derision in Revil's smile while he continued to observe her intently. 'You have to work at it all the time, and quite often you fail,' she added, thinking of her own dismal failure at finding happiness.

'Happiness is a commodity which comes with the contentment of the soul, and to achieve that contentment one must be true not only to oneself, but also to others,' Revil pointed out, and Alexa felt her heart contract with compassion when, for one brief moment, his features bore the look of a man who was torn between his loyalty to his sister and the result of his own perceptive observations.

'What's happening out at Izilwane, Byron?' Vivien O'Brien changed the subject, and Alexa drew a slow, steadying breath to ease the tension inside her.

'The building operations have progressed favourably since the last time you were there,' Byron smiled, his tawny eyes crinkling at the corners as he stretched his long, khaki-clad legs out in front of him. 'What about taking a drive out to Izilwane some time in the near future?'

'I'll do that as soon as I can catch my husband somewhere between his consulting hours and duties at the hospital,' Vivien O'Brien said with a rueful grimace. 'He's been so busy lately, but our lives will settle down again to comparative normality as soon as his partner returns from a much deserved holiday.'

Byron nodded understandingly. 'I shall look forward, then, to your visit.'

'You caused quite a stir in the district when you decided to start a game park, but I think we needed something like that to put Louisville on the map.' Vivien O'Brien's dark eyes surveyed Byron curiously. 'Is it true that you're going to introduce lion into the park at some future date?'

'It's true,' he nodded, smiling wryly, 'but it won't be for another year or so.'

'I hope you've provided adequate fencing, or you'll have the ranchers breathing fire at you if they have any stock losses.' Vivien O'Brien laughed, but there was an obvious hint of warning in her voice.

'The only way the animals could escape from the park would be if someone was stupid enough to cut the fences, and I don't envisage that problem.' Byron's smile was confident. 'The ranchers are as anxious to keep their cattle where they belong as I am to keep my animals in the park.'

Dr Peter O'Brien arrived home a few minutes later, and his wife poured him a cup of tea as he settled his tall, lean frame tiredly in a chair. Fair-haired and blue-eyed like his daughter Megan, and with that inevitable smell of antiseptic clinging to his clothes, he chatted amiably and listened with pride and interest when he was told of the offer Revil had made Megan.

'I'm very happy for you, sweetheart,' Peter O'Brien smiled at his daughter, but his smile changed to a grimace when the telephone started ringing shrilly in the hall. 'If that's for me, then tell them I'm not at home.'

Vivien O'Brien's smile was a mixture of concern and sympathy when she rose to answer the telephone, but when she returned to the living-room a few seconds later it was Byron to whom she spoke.

'You're needed rather urgently out at Izilwane, Byron,' she passed on the message which had been given to her. 'It appears they are having problems again at the water plant.'

'Damn!' Byron muttered with some annoyance, rising abruptly to his feet. 'I thought I'd sorted that problem out yesterday, but apparently I haven't.'

Alexa deposited a sleepy Pickles in Megan O'Brien's arms, and they left the O'Brien residence a few minutes later to return to Izilwane at a speed that made her fear for their lives at times, but Byron was an excellent driver, and the Land Rover held the road as if it were glued to it.

The afternoon spent with Megan O'Brien and her family had been extremely pleasant and enjoyable, notwithstanding those few unhappy exchanges which Alexa didn't wish to dwell on. They were the nicest people she had met in a long, long time. They had generated a genuine warmth and friendliness which had touched her to the core, and she knew that she would never forget it.

CHAPTER EIGHT

ALEXA could not shake off that distressing sensation that she was experiencing a period of calmness before the inevitable storm. She had feared the remainder of the weekend at Izilwane, and she had also feared that brooding quality in Revil's eyes whenever he thought she was not looking, but he had kept his distance like a polite and amiable stranger. She had hoped that her uneasiness would diminish after their return to Johannesburg, but instead it had grown.

She had seen Revil only briefly during the ten days following that weekend at Izilwane, but his cool and distant behaviour did not encourage conversation, and she was beginning to discover that this was the most painful punishment of all. She had had some idea of what to expect when they had been together, but his silence and his absence was not only nerve-racking, it was sharpening her longing for him with an intensity she had difficulty in controlling at times.

Madame Véronique had made her models work until they had come close to dropping with fatigue, but none of them had objected. The fashion show was two days away. They had worked hard, but they were looking forward to it, and at the banquet hall in the Carlton Centre they were able to put all their hard work into practice for the final dress-rehearsal.

They worked their way steadily through the eye-catching and fashionable outfits André Dacre had designed for the coming spring, and then came the finale; the full-length wedding-gown in pure white satin trimmed with a misty imported lace.

Alexa had practised her routine often enough, but she felt distinctly odd on this occasion when she stepped out behind the curtains and walked slowly down the length of the low, thickly carpeted platform. Her mind was a jumble of thoughts, none of them constructive, but she could feel that she was not projecting the required image, and she could see it in the gravity of Madame's expression when her routine came to an end.

'Ah, yes, Alexa, that was very good,' Madame Véronique nodded with a measure of approval, 'but I would like you to try it once again. You know the routine well enough, but this time I want you to clear your mind of everything except the knowledge that you are the radiant bride, and you are walking into the church to become the wife of the man you love.' Madame smiled, a query in her dark eyes. 'Could you do that, *chérie*?'

'I'll try, Madame,' Alexa nodded, returning to her position behind the curtains to repeat her routine.

She was only vaguely aware of the rest of the models hovering in the background, and she closed her eyes for a moment to concentrate. What was it Madame Véronique had said? *You are the radiant bride, and you are walking into the church to become the wife of the man you love.*

Pain wrenched at her heart like the savage beak of a vulture ripping at tender flesh, and she had to bite back the cry of anguish that rose to her lips. Madame did not know what she was asking her to do. She would never know the personal joy of marrying the man she loved. Revil would never love her in return, and marriage was not something he would ever list on the agenda for his future.

Alexa drew a deep, steadying breath to calm herself. She had to forget about Revil. For those few brief minutes, when she would be wearing André Dacre's magnificent creation, she would have to banish Revil's harsh, mocking features from her mind, and she would have to pretend that the impossible had happened.

It had taken but a few seconds for Alexa to prepare herself mentally and, when she stepped out behind the curtain for the second time, there was a radiance emanating from her which was clearly visible to all who stood watching her, but they would never know how many tears she was shedding on the inside. She recalled to mind the fondness in the warm smile Revil had bestowed on Carol Ross, and she clung to that memory, her mouth curving in a shy, expectant response while her slender body moved with a proud, natural grace that made it appear as if she were floating rather than walking across the wine-red carpet. She turned slowly at the end of the platform, the misty veil adding a touch of mystery to her ethereal appearance as she calmly retraced her steps, and paused, turning to her left, and then to her right for the last time before she returned to her required position where the deep blue of the velvet curtains was a perfect foil for André Dacre's outstanding creativity as a couturier.

Silence greeted the completion of Alexa's routine; a silence which was loaded with a vibrancy which finally exploded into applause from the rest of the girls in the wings as well as the man and the woman standing at the end of the platform.

'Excellent, *chérie*! *Magnifique*!' Madame Véronique exclaimed, her dark eyes alight with excitement when she stepped on to the platform and walked towards Alexa with André Dacre following close behind her. 'What is your opinion, Monsieur Dacre?'

'I could not have expressed my feelings more accurately than you have, Madame Véronique,' he smiled broadly, taking Alexa's right hand between his slender fingers and raising it to his lips. 'You *were* magnificent, my dear, and if you model my wedding-gown tomorrow evening the way you did now, then I can almost guarantee you a standing ovation.'

Alexa's facial muscles had stiffened like the leg muscles of a long-distance runner at the end of a race, and she had to force her lips into a smile. 'The credit is yours, Mr Dacre.'

'Don't be so modest, my dear Alexa,' he admonished her at once, releasing her hand to gesture impatiently. 'I have created a magnificent wedding-gown, and I have not the slightest desire to be modest about it, so I don't see why you should be modest about the fact that you have the natural style and grace to model my creation to perfection. It is a team effort,' he added, regarding her closely. 'Do you accept that?'

Alexa considered this for a moment. Praise from André Dacre was indeed worth having, and this time it took a little less effort to smile. 'I accept that, and I'm honoured.'

There was an air of quivering excitement amongst the models, and it was clearly evident in their raised voices when Madame entered the dressing-room half an hour later with Bradstone's creative director.

'Ladies, may I have your attention, please?' The lean, sparsely built man had to raise his voice above the excited clamour to receive the silence he desired for the announcement he obviously had to make. 'We have a session lined up for you at the Izilwane Game Park in the northern Transvaal,' he enlightened them. 'There will be a photographer and a camera crew for the television commercials to advertise the park and its facilities, and we're throwing in a couple of male models just for good measure.'

So Revil had taken her suggestion seriously after all, Alexa thought, a faint smile easing the tightness about her mouth while the rest of the girls squealed with delight at the prospect of male models being present during this assignment.

'We have chartered a flight for this coming Saturday,' he enlightened them. 'It will leave the Rand airport at nine o'clock the morning, and work will begin on the Monday.'

'How long will we be expected to stay at this what's-its-name park?' Lucille questioned him.

'Izilwane.' The creative director provided the name of the game park with an indulgent smile. 'It will take us a couple of days to get the necessary shots, but, at a guess, I should say you'll be back in Johannesburg by the following weekend.' He cast a sweeping glance across the room. 'Any further questions?'

'What will we be modelling?' Lucille questioned him again.

'This is not a modelling assignment as such,' the creative director explained. 'You will naturally receive a wardrobe of suitable outfits which you will be expected to wear, but the purpose of this session is specifically to introduce the game park and its facilities to the public, and to do it in such a way that they will feel compelled to pay it a visit during their next holiday.'

He answered a few more questions, and then they were free to go home for that much needed rest before the actual night of the fashion show.

Alexa was looking forward to this second trip to Izilwane. Being part of a group would allow for a more relaxed atmosphere, but first there was André Dacre's spring collection she had to concentrate on, and the presentation had to be made without a fault.

Alexa was jittery, and for the first time in her professional life she had difficulty in concealing it. Her hands were shaking almost as much as her insides, and she dropped the diamanté studded combs twice before she succeeded in securing them in her hair.

This was not simply an ordinary fashion show. It was the first of the two most important fashion shows of the year for André Dacre under the banner of Bradstone Promotions, and its success depended not only on the couturier's creations, but on the expertise of Madame Véronique's models. Amongst those attending the show would be people of importance in the fashion world, the various members of the press, and the television crew manning their cameras to give live coverage of this glittering occasion. If Alexa could wish herself anywhere at that moment, she would wish herself up in the northern Transvaal where she could bask in the peace and tranquillity of Izilwane.

Excitement, and a certain amount of expectancy, hovered in the air that evening amongst the scantily clad models in the dressing-room. Madame Véronique flitted amongst them, looking outwardly calm, but showing visible signs of nervous strain about the eyes and mouth. She had trained them rigorously, she knew they would give of their very best, but there was always the chance that an error might slip in unnoticed.

Alexa was applying her mascara when Madame warned, 'You have five minutes, *mes enfants*. Listen for your cue, and good luck.'

Five minutes! Alexa's heart was beating in her throat and drumming loudly in her ears. She rose quickly like everyone else, and slipped into the required outfit. The clock against the wall was ticking away the seconds, faster and faster, and then they received the call they had all been waiting for. It was time to go on.

She stood in the wings with Lucille, listening to Madame's deceptively calm and faintly accented voice as she spoke into the microphone. Her glance met Lucille's for one brief second, and she glimpsed in Lucille's eyes the same anxiety which was knotting her nerves painfully at the pit of her stomach.

'This is it!' Lucille whispered, and Alexa sent up a brief, silent prayer a fraction of a second before they stepped out behind the curtains and into the spotlight.

No one watching the two models doing their routine on the platform would have guessed that they were nervous and barely aware of anything other than the task they were performing. Their features were calm, their movements fluid and relaxed, and they smiled, almost provocatively at times, while their glances blindly encompassed everyone in the banquet hall.

The applause, when they had done their turn, was like music to Alexa's ears. The worst was over, her nerves had begun to unravel themselves into a reasonable form of normality, and she found that she could actually relax and enjoy herself to some extent as the evening wore on.

Revil was in the audience, she had seen him seated close to the platform with several other dignitaries and, as usual, he looked devastating in formal evening dress. His presence had not disturbed her except for that familiar quickening of her pulse, and, though she might have imagined it, she could almost swear that he had smiled at her once without that ever present mockery in his eyes.

Everything had gone smoothly and, at last, the finale was at hand. The background music changed to something more sedate, and Alexa drew a steadying breath behind the curtains before she stepped out in full view of the audience. An appreciative murmur erupted, and then there was silence as Alexa, her mind centred on

the advice Madame Véronique had given her, walked
slowly down the length of the carpeted platform. She did
not look at Revil, she dared not, but she could feel his
eyes burning into her when she turned slowly at the end
of the platform and retraced her steps.

Alexa could feel her insides shaking when she finally
took up her position against the deep blue velvet
curtains, and, on the dais nearby, Madame Véronique
smiled at her with a trace of tears in her brown eyes.
Madame approved, but the ensuing silence terrified
Alexa, and then she received the highest honour any
model could wish for. The audience rose as one to their
feet, and the applause that followed was almost
deafening.

Tears of relief filled Alexa's eyes, but she blinked them
away hastily, her glance searching eagerly for Revil,
and a wave of coldness swept through her. His chair was
empty, and she paled as if he had literally slapped her
through the face.

André Dacre appeared in the wings, and Alexa pulled
herself together hastily. She held out her hand to him,
and the applause rose to a climax when he stepped out
behind the curtains to join her on the platform. His
slender fingers closed about hers, and he bowed low to
acknowledge the applause, then he turned and, much to
the delight of the audience, he raised Alexa's hand to his
lips.

'Didn't I promise you a standing ovation?' he
whispered to her with a twinkle in his eyes, and Alexa's
answering smile hid the pain which was tearing through
her.

It was some time before Alexa was allowed to return
to the dressing-room, but she almost had to fight her way
through a barrage of photographers and newsmen.
Cameras flashed, almost blinding her, and questions

were rapped out at her which she was not given time to answer. Business cards, accompanied by fantastic offers from several international magazines, were thrust into her hands, and when at last she was allowed to escape into the dressing-room she sagged with fatigue, but it was not over yet. A group of seven girls, with Lucille in the lead, stormed at Alexa, kissing and hugging her in their excitement. Their morale was high, and it was some time before their excitement died down, but Alexa had never felt lower.

'I don't deserve all the praise,' Alexa protested. 'We all worked very hard to make this fashion show a success, and we all deserve the acclaim, but most of all I feel Madame Véronique ought to be praised for what she has made of us.'

'You're too modest, Alexa,' they brushed aside her remarks. 'We agree that Madame deserves to be praised, but we all know that you're the best, and we're happy for you.'

Alexa turned from them with a lump in her throat, and their excited chatter continued while Lucille quietly helped Alexa out of the wedding-gown. The dressing-room emptied slowly until there was no one left except Lucille and Alexa.

'Are you staying for the party?' asked Lucille, and Alexa shook her head.

'No, I'm going home.'

'You really did deserve all the praise you received this evening,' Lucille insisted, then she gestured towards the business cards Alexa was dropping unceremoniously into her handbag. 'Are you going to accept any of those offers?'

'I don't think so—I don't know, I—' Alexa pressed her fingers against her throbbing temples. 'Lucille, I am just too tired to think straight.'

Lucille nodded, and a speculative look suddenly entered her eyes. 'Carol Ross was here this evening, and I saw Revil Bradstone chatting her up a few minutes ago.'

'Is that so?' murmured Alexa, feeling strangely numb as she put on her coat and rummaged through her handbag.

'Doesn't it bother you?'

'What bothers me at the moment is that I can't seem to find my car keys,' Alexa answered her without looking up.

'I think I heard something jingling in your coat pocket.'

'What? Oh, yes,' she muttered, her fingers closing about the small bunch of keys in her pocket and, picking up her handbag, she forced her unwilling lips into a smile when she glanced at her friend. 'Goodnight, Lucille.'

They left the dressing-room together, Lucille to join the party, and Alexa going in the opposite direction along the dimly lit passage which led to the side entrance. She had walked only a few paces when she stopped abruptly, and her heart lurched violently in her breast.

Revil was waiting for her at the far end of the long, shadowy passage. Dark and handsome, and with that undeniable element of danger in his stance, his presence excited as well as frightened her. A breathless eternity seemed to pass before she was capable of setting herself in motion again, but every beat of her heart was like a painful drum hammering against her temples.

'Aren't you staying to celebrate the success of the show?' he asked when she paused a pace or two away from him, and there was an unmistakable hint of mockery in his voice that tugged cruelly at her raw, tense nerves.

'I'd rather go home.'

'There are people out there clamouring to meet you, and Carol was hoping you would join us for the remainder of the evening.'

She shrank inwardly at the mere idea of having to confront anyone else that evening, most of all Carol Ross, and she shook her head adamantly. 'Some other time, perhaps.'

'Oh, don't put on this act of the shy celebrity with me!' he mocked her. 'What could possibly be more exhilarating than staying to celebrate your success this evening, or do you have something ... or someone waiting at home for you?' His eyes glittered suddenly like chips of ice. 'Is that why you're in such a hurry to leave?'

Alexa went hot, then cold, and pain mingled with disgust in her eyes when she turned away from him. 'Goodnight, Revil.'

'Not so fast.' Fingers of steel were clamped about her arm, hurting her through the thickness of her coat. 'I'll see you out to your car.'

Tiredness and a terrible tightness across her chest prevented her from shrugging him off, and she allowed herself to be ushered out of the building to where she had parked her car. He held out his hand for her keys and unlocked the door for her, but his hand gripped her shoulder, preventing her from getting into her car.

'Is there someone waiting for you at home?' he demanded, his narrowed, probing glance holding hers captive beneath the light in the car park, and she shook her head in a negative reply when she found that her throat was too tight to speak.

Revil's hand settled in the hollow of her back, and she was drawn towards him until she rested unwillingly against the hard length of his body. His mouth swooped down on hers with a demanding, hungry passion to which she responded instinctively, but it left her drained and swaying weakly on her feet when he finally released her.

'Goodnight, Alexa.' He smiled down into her bewildered eyes, then he strode back into the building without giving her so much as a backward glance.

Alexa was shivering as she slumped into the driver's seat and closed the door. She felt as if she were on a mental see-saw, and she was not quite sure how to interpret a kiss which had followed so swiftly on a hurtful accusation. What was he trying to do to her? For two weeks he had practically ignored her, and now this! She was hovering somewhere between laughter and tears, but she was determined to give way to neither. '*Dammit!*' she swore loudly, slamming her clenched fist against the steering wheel, and the physical pain stabbing into her wrist sobered her to some extent, but she sat staring blindly ahead of her for several seconds before she felt capable of driving herself back to her flat.

The telephone rang at nine the following morning in Alexa's flat, and she sat up in bed with a start only to groan and clutch her head the next instant. It had taken her hours to fall asleep, and her headache of the night before seemed worse this morning. If only the telephone would stop ringing! The shrill, piercing sound seemed to stab repeatedly like a knife entering her brain, but the only way she could silence that punishing sound was to get up out of bed and stagger into the lounge.

She snatched up the receiver, stunned for a moment by the blessed silence, then she lifted the offending instrument to her ear and said irritably, 'Hello, who is that?'

'I want to see you, Alexa.' Revil's harsh, authoritative voice stabbed into her sensitive ear. 'I want you here at my office at ten o'clock sharp this morning.'

Alexa drew an angry breath, but the line went dead before she could answer him, and she sagged against the wall, slamming the receiver back on to its cradle in a fit of pent-up frustration and fury.

'*Damn you, Revil!*' she cried out, raising her fists to the white, concrete ceiling, but the effort simply aggravated her headache, and she was forced to go into the bathroom to swallow down a couple of pain-killers.

Why did Revil want to see her in his office? What was he going to accuse her of this time? Oh, God, was this torture never going to end?

The fierce desire to ignore Revil's abrupt call was hastily suppressed. He had not made a request, he had issued an instruction, and something in his voice had warned her not to disobey him. She had an hour to get dressed and to present herself in his office at the Bradstone building, and she had sensed that Revil was not in a mood to be tolerant if she should arrive late.

She bathed as quickly as she could, and her headache had receded by the time she had dressed herself warmly in pale blue slacks with a matching jacket. It was a bleak day with clouds hanging low in the wintry sky which promised no rain, but it reflected her emotional state aptly, she thought some time later when she was driving towards Bradstone's.

Alexa entered the spacious foyer at Bradstone Promotions at exactly five minutes to ten. The grandeur of the place no longer filled her with awe, and she had seen the potted palms and tinkling fountains often enough during the past gruelling weeks to pass them without actually noticing them. She walked towards the lifts, and thumbed the button. The lift doors slid open,

and she stepped into that plush, steel cage with as much
trepidation as she had done that very first time when *she*
had made an appointment to meet Revil. It all seemed so
long ago, and yet it was four weeks to the day that she
had dared to confront Revil in his office and question
him as to whether Madame Véronique would receive
the contract she had desired so much.

The lift doors slid shut silently, and she was swept up
to the twenty-second floor with a speed which still gave
her that awful feeling that she had left a vital part of her
behind on the ground floor.

Revil's secretary looked up from her typewriter a few
seconds later, and she smiled that pretty smile when she
saw Alexa walking towards her, but this time Alexa did
not have to give her name.

'You may go in, Miss Drew,' she announced, and
Alexa steeled herself mentally for this meeting with
Revil as she tapped lightly on the panelled door and
opened it.

Revil was seated behind his desk and he looked up
sharply, his smoke-grey glance narrowing slightly as it
trailed over her and took in every detail of her
appearance. 'Close the door and sit down.'

Alexa closed the door and turned, but she had gone
only a few paces across the thickly carpeted floor when
she froze as if she had suddenly been chiselled out of a
block of ice. Hanging against the pale grey wall, where
Revil would have no difficulty in seeing it, was Megan
O'Brien's pencil sketch of Alexa, and Alexa was
convinced that it was not hanging there for the usual
reasons a man would keep a photograph, or a portrait of
a woman in his office.

'Why did you do it? Why is that sketch framed and
hanging here in your office?' The words were wrung
from her as if there was a part of her that welcomed the

pain which she feared his answer would inflict upon her, and there was bitterness in the soft curve of her mouth when she dragged her anguished gaze from the sketch to look at Revil. 'Do you need to be reminded daily of how much you despise me?'

'I need to be reminded daily that artists, like animals, are very perceptive where people are concerned,' he corrected, smiling faintly. 'Young Megan O'Brien is an exceptional artist with a very discerning eye.'

Her insides jolted as if Revil had whipped the carpet from under her feet. How was she supposed to interpret that remark? she wondered, staring at him speechlessly until her legs threatened to cave in beneath her, and she sat down hastily to face Revil across the wide expanse of his cluttered desk. 'Why did you want to see me, Revil?'

He leaned back in his chair, his eyes narrowed to unfathomable slits, the expensive cut of his dark jacket accentuating the width of his powerful shoulders.

'Was the latter half of your evening as successful as the first half?' Alexa's insides lurched sickeningly, and she was parting her lips to draw a startled breath when he raised his hand imperiously. 'Don't answer that!' he barked at her, his mouth tightening with a savage twist. 'I'd rather believe that you spent the rest of the evening alone.'

'Revil, for God's sake!' she pleaded, her face ashen as she lifted a trembling hand to her throat. 'I wish you would believe me and end this nightmare I have to endure day and night!'

He rose abruptly, his expression strangely tortured as he turned his back on her to look out of the window, and Alexa sensed that he was fighting a fierce battle with himself while she looked on helplessly, loving the way his hair grew strongly into his neck and fighting against her own desperate longing to touch him.

She had long since relinquished the attempt to understand herself. She knew that Revil could never care for her, and yet she still had this incredible desire to touch him, to hold him ... and to love him. Dear heaven! She was wasting away her emotions on a man who did not deserve them, and if she had to be analysed she would most probably be told that she was crazy, but she could not help it. She loved him, it was as simple as that.

'It seems as though you have a very good chance of getting what you want after all.' His harsh voice sliced into her thoughts, and she stared at him blankly when he turned to face her with a mocking, faintly cynical smile playing about his sensuous mouth.

'What are you talking about?' she asked, and he waved a hand towards the newspapers lying on his desk.

'You are being acclaimed by some as the *Model of the Year*, but that's not all.' His mocking smile deepened. 'A visiting French couturier is obviously very keen to whisk you away to his fashion house in Paris.'

She sat there staring at him, her face a cool, uninterested mask behind which she concealed her feelings. Had she heard this news from someone else she might have felt flattered, perhaps even a little excited, but, coming from Revil, she was inclined to see it as yet another weapon with which he could attack and destroy her if he wished.

'It all sounds fantastic and very exciting, but nothing will come of it.' Her voice was cold and tainted with such a bitter sarcasm that she barely recognised it as her own. 'You'll see to that, won't you?'

'Success is lurking around the corner,' he persisted, ignoring her remark and watching her intently while he resumed his seat behind the desk. 'How badly do you want to reach out and grasp it?'

This was a trap. He was holding out what he considered was the bait, and he expected her to snap it up. Oh, he was clever. *Very* clever. But she had no intention of taking that carefully baited hook.

'I have never aspired to international acclaim,' she answered him calmly and cautiously, and also with a considerable amount of that honesty he did not believe she possessed. 'I shall consider it an honour if it comes my way, but I doubt if I shall accept it.'

'What *do* you want out of life, Alexa?' he demanded, using the direct approach where his subtlety had failed. 'What do you desire the most?'

'Happiness ... to a certain degree,' she confounded him, 'but I'll settle for contentment.'

'Happiness and contentment,' he repeated slowly, leaning forward to rest his arms on the desk blotter. 'Do you desire happiness and contentment in your work, or are you hoping to find it in marriage to some idiot who's crazy enough to want to give up his freedom?'

Alexa winced inwardly. There had been no need for Revil to underline the fact that he would never exchange his freedom for marriage, and least of all would he do that for her.

'I doubt if I shall ever marry,' she confessed, lowering her gaze to her tightly clenched hands in her lap. 'My work has become important to me, but my idea of success is having a modelling agency of my own one day.'

That was yet another dream which she was beginning to doubt would ever come true, and during the ensuing silence the atmosphere between them became packed with tension.

'My sister will be returning to South Africa in two weeks' time.' Revil's voice had an ominous ring to it, and she looked up sharply to see him frowning down at the blotter on his desk. 'I want to arrange a meeting between

the two of you, and I want it to occur as soon as possible
after Wilma's return.'

'I look forward to meeting her.'

'Do you?'

A strained silence prevailed while they faced each
other across his desk, but it was during this silence that
Alexa realised the enormity of what she had agreed to. If
Revil had begun to doubt Wilma in recent weeks, and
Alexa had sensed that doubt in him on several occasions,
then a meeting between the three of them would destroy
the remnants of his faith in his sister, and Alexa could
not bear the thought of being the instrument of such
destruction.

'*Dammit*, Revil!' she snapped, her eyes blazing with a
fury which was directed at no one in particular. 'Did you
make me come here this morning for the sole purpose of
informing me of your sister's arrival in two weeks' time?
Couldn't you have told me that on the telephone?'

An unfathomable expression flitted across the harsh
angles and planes of Revil's face, and an equally
unfathomable smile curved his strong, sensuous mouth.

'There are certain things which cannot be said on a
telephone, and since I'm flying to Cape Town this
evening it will be days before I have the opportunity to
discuss something of importance with you.'

'What is there to discuss which is of such importance?'
she asked, holding her breath with the odd feeling that
Revil had raised an axe above her head.

'I'm referring to this.' He gestured towards the folded
newspapers on his desk. 'I want you to know that I have
plans for you which might not necessarily coincide with
what you had in mind for yourself, so don't get too
excited about these articles in the newspaper.'

Shock waves rippled across her tender nerves and
coiled them into agonising knots. She had feared this, he

had threatened to ruin her often enough, but for some peculiar reason she had thought that he had discarded the idea along with several other preconceived notions he had had about her, and the pain of knowing that she had been mistaken was tearing savagely at her soul. He had said that he would have his revenge *if* the final analysis demanded it. What had made him change his mind?

'Thanks for the warning,' she retaliated sarcastically, her face a white, rigid mask as she rose to her feet with as much dignity as she could muster. 'Do I have your permission to leave now?'

'You may go,' he smiled twistedly, 'and enjoy this coming week at Izilwane. It may well be your last assignment for Madame Véronique, because you and I are going to have a serious discussion on your return.'

Alexa's nerves reacted as if she had been connected to a high-voltage wire. Her hands tightened convulsively on the back of the chair until her knuckles whitened, and her eyes were like crushed violets in her ashen face when she stared at Revil. Her mind leapt about wildly while she assimilated the facts and accepted them numbly, but her heart refused to believe that the man she loved . . .!

A smothered sound escaped past her lips as she turned and walked out of his office. She was blinded by tears, and she was never quite sure afterwards how she managed to reach her car in the car park without a mishap occurring along the way.

CHAPTER NINE

THE trip to Izilwane, and the reason for it, was an entirely new experience for Alexa. The camera became the audience—a tolerant audience that did not object when they made a mistake and the action had to be repeated. The days were so hot that most of the photographs had to be taken in the shade, but the nights were cool, and ideal for sitting around an outside fire making *braaivleis* and discussing the programme for the following day in a relaxed atmosphere. This was a bitter-sweet assignment for Alexa. It was her last, if she could believe Revil, and she did.

Izilwane. Animal. A perfect name for a game park, and a perfect setting for it as well, Alexa decided, sighing as she leaned back against a tree and watched the smoke curling upwards from the fire. Man and beast shared the peace and tranquillity, and at night they shared the blanket of stars, stars that were so bright they seemed close enough to touch.

Byron Rockford had joined them every night around the fire. He would keep them enthralled with tales of exciting and sometimes frightening incidents in other parks where he had been a game warden, and he would tell them about the various animals and their habits, but Alexa suspected his presence was mainly to keep a watchful eye on the fire to make sure that it was doused properly before they all went to bed. Fire was the enemy of man as well as beast. A careless spark shooting into the dry winter veld could start an inferno, and the results could be horrific.

Alexa's casual glance trailed across the group seated about the fire. Two men and two women made up the television camera crew and the photographer. Besides them there were four male models to Madame Véronique's eight girls. 'Goody, we have a fifty-fifty chance!' Lucille had shrieked excitedly on their arrival at Izilwane, but Alexa had countered with an icy, 'Count me out!' Her last encounter with Revil had left her bruised and considerably shaken, and her future, *if* she had a future, was suddenly terribly uncertain. Would she still have a job when she returned to Johannesburg?

Enjoy this coming week at Izilwane. It may well be your last assignment for Madame Véronique.

Damn Revil! If only she *could* relax and enjoy herself in these beautiful surroundings, but he had made that quite impossible. He had done more than simply threaten her future, he was going to axe it completely, and she no longer doubted that she would soon have to walk the streets looking for something suitable to do to earn a decent living. Perhaps that would appease him. Perhaps then . . .

Alexa sighed heavily. There was no sense in hoping for miracles. Her heart was reaching out for something which would never be there for her, and she had to stop tormenting herself this way, or she would go insane!

She went to bed early that night. She had been feeling listless and lethargic since their arrival at the game park, and it had been growing steadily worse. She had tried to excuse her mental and physical attitude to Lucille by saying that the heat was draining her of her energy, but she knew that the heat had absolutely nothing to do with the way she felt. She awoke some nights to find herself drenched in perspiration and her cheeks damp with tears she didn't recall shedding, and on those occasions she was thankful that she had a one-bedroomed bungalow to herself.

The Wednesday morning of that week at Izilwane was as hot and humid as all the other days, and Alexa could feel the perspiration breaking out all over her body long before it was her turn to step in front of the cameras. She was wearing blue shorts with a safari type blouse of a matching colour, and her feet were shod in colourful rope sandals. They left the camp at dawn with two of Byron Rockford's game wardens accompanying them through the park to ensure their safety while they were photographed in Land Rovers with binoculars slung about their necks, or raised to their eyes in search of animals amongst the trees. The theme bordered on the romantic, and they were required to point enthusiastically, smile gaily, or gaze into the eyes of a male model, but they were not always successful in capturing some of the animals in the background.

It was ten-thirty that morning when they arrived back at the camp. There was time to have something cool to drink, and then the work continued, but this time the photographic session was to take place in and around the main building.

Alexa was leaning against one of the wooden pillars supporting the thatched roof of the patio, and Cedric, one of the male models, was standing behind her, his hand on her shoulder, and his head lowered as if he was going to kiss her slender neck. It was then that Alexa caught a glimpse of Megan O'Brien observing the proceedings from a distance. They waved briefly at each other, but the camera continued clicking away.

'Hello, Miss Drew.' Megan O'Brien greeted Alexa with her warm smile a few minutes later during a short break when Alexa joined her beside her small white Mazda parked in the shade of a mopani tree.

'Please call me Alexa.'

'Alexa,' Megan repeated obligingly, her blue, curious gaze meeting Alexa's. 'Is it short for Alexandra?'

Alexa shook her head and smiled faintly at this familiar query. 'No, it's just Alexa.'

'Your job must be terribly exciting,' Megan announced, her eyes sparkling with interest as she cast a glance in the direction where the photographic session was still in progress.

'It merely looks that way,' Alexa assured her.

'It certainly did from where I was standing,' Megan sighed affectedly. 'All those magnificent-looking men cuddling up to you, even if it is only for the camera's sake, and I really don't know how you manage to stay so cool and calm. I know I wouldn't be able to do that. I'd be in a constant swoon.'

'Oh, Megan!' Alexa's laughter drew several surprised glances of which she was oblivious. 'We're much too busy trying to acquire the perfect pose for the camera to think of swooning.'

'I wish I could have done a painting of you as you are now.' Megan's remark startled Alexa into silence. 'When you laugh your eyes sparkle like rare jewels,' Megan explained, 'and there's no sign of the sadness I've seen lurking there.'

Megan's keen, perceptive glance was unnerving, and Alexa hastily changed the subject. 'How has your own work been progressing?'

'I've just delivered a batch of paintings for Mr Bradstone's approval,' Megan informed her. 'Byron told me that Mr Bradstone would be flying up to Izilwane this afternoon, and if he approves of the first batch, then I'll continue with the rest.'

Alexa's heart lurched as she turned to stare at Megan

in surprise. 'Revil Bradstone is flying up to Izilwane this afternoon?'

'Yes,' Megan nodded, her honey-gold curls bobbing about her head. 'Didn't he tell you?'

'No, I——' Alexa's voice broke, and she halted abruptly to clear her throat before she tried again. 'He never said anything.'

'Byron could have told you, but—oh, dear!' Megan looked distressed and grimly apologetic. 'Perhaps his arrival this afternoon was intended as a surprise for you, and now I've gone and spoiled it by opening my big mouth!'

'Don't worry about it, Megan.' Alexa smiled wryly, regaining a fraction of her composure. 'I doubt that his arrival was intended as a surprise.'

His unexpected arrival might have been planned to unnerve and disorientate her, but *never* as a pleasant surprise; Alexa was quite convinced about that.

'Alexa!' She looked up sharply to see the phototgrapher gesturing to her. 'We need to do a few more shots here!'

'Coming!' Alexa called back, then she turned apologetically to the young woman beside her. 'I have to go, but it was nice meeting you again, Megan, and do pass on my regards to your parents.'

'Thanks, I'll do that,' Megan smiled, getting into her car. 'I'm hoping we'll meet again, so I'll just say *tot siens*.'

Alexa nodded, and she waited until Megan had driven away before she walked across to where the photographer was waiting rather impatiently for her.

They left the camp again late that afternoon and headed out towards the dam for a sunset cruise on a motor-driven launch. The water lapping against the sides of the launch and the throbbing of the engines would not have detracted from this idyllic cruise, but they were not there for the pleasure of it. The television camera rolled, the photographer snapped away, and instructions were being fired at the models from all angles. There was no time to enjoy the sight of the animals gathering in herds at the water's edge at that time of day, as was their habit, and Alexa felt a stab of regret at the knowledge that she might never be given the opportunity again to observe the animals in their natural habitat.

The sun was setting like a red ball of fire in the sky, and it was tinting the fleecy clouds with pink and gold when they finally began the return journey to the camp. Their work was on schedule, and everyone was in a particularly jovial mood, but Alexa could feel herself flagging. She needed a shower and a change of clothing, but, more than that, she needed an extra burst of stamina to cope with Revil when they met, as they undoubtedly would.

Revil was talking to Byron outside the main building when they arrived at the camp, and Alexa's heart seemed to somersault in her breast at the mere sight of him standing there. Revil had his shirt sleeves rolled up to his elbows, his tie had been loosened, and the jacket of his dark grey business suit was draped casually over one arm. He had obviously arrived only a few minutes prior to their return to the camp, judging by the briefcase in his hand and the overnight bag at his feet, and Alexa shrank back nervously against her seat when he cast a brief, searching glance in their direction before he walked away along the path to the bungalows, leaving Byron to saunter towards them.

'The restaurant is still in the process of being enlarged, but I've arranged for you to have dinner there this evening,' Byron told them when they emerged from the Land Rovers. 'Afterwards we could shift the tables and chairs to one side, and if I manage to lay my hands on a few decent records you could have yourselves an impromptu ball.'

The group cheered enthusiastically, but Alexa couldn't match their enthusiasm. She would have preferred their usual evening around the fire where she could have positioned herself in the shadows to remain unnoticed, but, unfortunately, she had no say in the matter.

It was dusk when Alexa walked along the flagstone path to her bungalow. She felt jittery and, for the first time since her arrival at Izilwane, she entered her bungalow and locked the door behind her. It was a ridiculous action, and she could not imagine what she was afraid of. There was nothing more Revil could do to hurt and destroy her. Was there?

She shivered despite the warmth of the night, and went into the bedroom to strip off her clothes. She would feel better after a shower and a change of clothing, but half an hour later she still laboured under that odd feeling that the axe had been raised above her head once again.

Alexa's cotton frock was a floral mixture of blue and green, with thin straps across smooth shoulders which had acquired a slight tan simply from being in the shade. She had left her hair down since it was still slightly damp after her shower, and it added a youthful touch to her appearance which drew wolf-whistles from the male members of the group when she entered the restaurant with its log-cabin décor and its low-hanging lights like old-fashioned lanterns.

She was blushing when she joined Lucille and two other girls at their table. Their teasing did not trouble her as much as the thought that Revil might have witnessed the incident when she entered the restaurant, but she relaxed when she cast a quick glance about the room to find that Revil was nowhere in sight.

Dinner that evening consisted of a wholesome tomato soup, roast lamb with fresh vegetables, and a fruit dessert with ice-cream. Everyone appeared to be in the right mood for a party as they finished off their meal with coffee, and when Byron arrived the men eagerly offered their assistance to shift the tables and chairs to clear a space in the centre of the restaurant for dancing.

The hi-fi equipment was set up in the corner of the room, and they discovered that Byron had a consider-able pile of records from which to make an appropriate selection for dancing. One of the young wardens had agreed to take charge of the hi-fi, and when the first record was placed on the turntable the floor was crowded with people eager to dance.

Alexa positioned herself out of the way in a corner of the room, content to watch rather than participate. Byron danced several dances with some of the girls, and when he finally appeared in front of Alexa, asking her to dance, she couldn't be impolite and refuse.

Byron, despite his massive build, was light on his feet, and his steps were easy to follow, but he was not a man for making inane conversation. He questioned her briefly about her work, she did the same about his, and then they lapsed into a comfortable silence to enjoy the remainder of the dance. When the record ended he did not release her, and they danced again, this time to a slow waltz.

Where was Revil? Not that it mattered, Alexa answered her own question. Much as she longed to see him, she would prefer it if he did not put in an appearance, but ... She had to stop caring! But *how*?

These thoughts had barely skipped through her mind when Alexa saw Revil entering the restaurant, and his mere presence disorientated her to such an extent that her step faltered.

'I'm sorry,' she muttered when Byron glanced down at her questioningly, and a slow smile creased his rugged features.

'Revil has that effect on some women when he walks into a room,' he said drily, and his perceptiveness sent a wave of heat surging into her cheeks that made his smile deepen with amusement.

'You've known each other a long time,' Alexa remarked when she had regained her composure to some extent.

'Yes, we have.' Byron confirmed what she had already known.

'Do you know his sister at all?' she dared to question him, but he gave no indication that her query surprised him.

'I know Wilma, but not as well as I know Revil.'

'What's she like?' Alexa persisted. 'As a person, I mean?'

'That's rather a difficult question to answer,' he smiled faintly, 'I've always thought of her as an unaffected, sincere woman, but appearances can be deceptive.'

'Revil is extremely fond of her.'

'He has always doted on her, even more so after the death of their parents, and the feeling is mutual, but I have, at times, had the odd suspicion that she's afraid of Revil.' Byron paused a moment, a frown creasing his brow before he continued. 'He became the head of the family and had to take over the family business at a very young age, and with it he assumed the responsibility as his sister's protector.' He smiled down at her suddenly. 'Does that answer your question?'

'In a way,' she answered his query casually, convinced that he had told her a lot more than he had actually intended to, and he had let something slip which might explain why Wilma had led her brother to believe, incorrectly, that Alexa had been the guilty party in that incident three years ago. 'Could this conversation remain between us?' she asked, raising her wary glance to his.

'I've forgotten it already,' Byron assured her with a smile, and she sighed inwardly, knowing instinctively that she could trust him.

'Thank you,' she murmured when the dance ended and Byron accompanied her back to her chair.

Revil was leaning against the wall close to the door. Alexa was aware of him, and she was aware also of his narrowed, smoke-grey glance following every move she made. It aroused a disquieting feeling to be observed like that, but she tried valiantly to ignore it.

The next record was placed on the turntable, and Alexa looked up to find Cedric standing in front of her. 'Shall we dance, Alexa?'

'This dance is mine, I think,' a frighteningly familiar voice said behind him, and Cedric stepped aside, preparing himself to question that statement, but he obviously decided that Revil was a formidable opponent, not to be tampered with lightly.

'Sure,' Cedric shrugged, conceding defeat, and walking away.

In brown slacks and a cream, short-sleeved shirt Revil exuded an aura of masculinity that sent her pulse-rate soaring. He held out his hand, imperious and commanding, and Alexa placed hers in it, allowing him to lead her on to the floor and take her into his arms as if she had no will of her own. His hand was resting against the hollow of her back, drawing her closer until his thighs brushed against hers while they danced to the slow beat of the music, and his nearness made the blood flow faster through her veins. Oh, if only he didn't have this devastating effect on her!

'Were you surprised to see me?' he questioned her.

'Nothing you do surprises me, Revil,' she answered with a calmness that belied the turmoil and the tension inside her. 'You always act true to form.'

'How dull you make me sound,' he smiled mockingly.

'Not dull,' she corrected with a hint of bitterness in her voice, 'but determined and relentless.'

'I like to know where I stand with people, and for that reason I let people know exactly where they stand with me.'

'An admirable quality, and I appreciate and admire it.'

'Do you?' he asked, looking dubious.

'Well, I've always known exactly where I stand with you, haven't I, Revil?' she said with a hint of sarcasm in her soft voice. 'You made it quite clear from the start what you thought of me, and at our last meeting you never hid the fact that you intend to ruin me regardless of the "final analysis" as you called it.' She raised her glance to his, hiding her pain and bitterness behind a smile. 'I ought really to be grateful to you for being so honest with me.'

His mouth tightened into a thin, angry line, and he spun her round towards the door. 'Let's get out of here.'

'Where are we going?' she demanded warily when he gripped her arm and marched her out of the building and along the flagstone path leading to the bungalows.

'We're going to a place where we can be alone.'

'But I don't want to be alone with you!' she protested, trying to free her arm from his vice-like grip, but succeeding only in hurting herself, and she had no option but to accompany him wherever he was taking her.

His features were hidden from her in the darkness, but she knew a sense of panic when he unlocked the door to a bungalow not far from her own and flicked the light switch just inside the door.

'Get inside,' he instructed, giving her a not-so-gentle push in the direction he wanted her to go, and Alexa found herself in a bungalow very similar to her own.

Revil closed the door and dropped the key on to a low table beside a chair. The smoky fire in his eyes lit an answering fire inside her. It made her feel uneasy and more than a little afraid when she realised that there was only one way he could still hurt her, but it was quite possible that, in the process, he might hurt himself. She didn't want him to make love to her, and she did not want to gain her freedom from his revenge by hurting him, even though he had hurt her so many times.

'I thought Izilwane might be the ideal place for that serious discussion I mentioned, but it seems I was wrong,' he said thickly. 'The discussion will have to wait.'

'Revil?' An anxious query was mirrored in her glance, and the smouldering fire in his eyes confirmed her suspicions. 'Don't do it,' she pleaded, a tremor in her voice with the effort to remain calm. 'Don't do something you'll regret afterwards.'

His hands framed her face, and she knew that, for her own sake, she had to do something, but her limbs refused to obey the frantic messages relayed from her mind. His thumbs brushed across her cheek bones, and she trembled when she felt the heat of his body through the cotton of her dress.

'I've waited too long, Alexa,' he murmured throatily, and his features were etched with lines of visible torment. 'I can't seem to get you out of my mind and out of my blood, and the agony of wanting you is driving me crazy.'

Her heart was beating in her throat, and making it difficult for her to breathe properly, let alone speak. Revil was going to kiss her; she knew he was going to kiss her and . . . oh, God, she wanted him to . . . she wanted it so very much! His warm breath mingled with hers before his mouth shifted over hers with a sensual passion that kindled the flame inside her and, for the moment, she was lost in the fathomless tide of emotion that swept through her.

He pushed his hands through her hair, making her scalp tingle, and she couldn't resist him when she felt his hand moving urgently down her back to draw her hips closer into the hard curve of his male body. If only it could always be like this, she thought, her arms moving of their own volition to become locked about his neck. If only he could love her instead of merely wanting her. If only he . . .

Don't be an idiot! she rebuked herself. There was absolutely no sense in wishing for the impossible. Revil desired her body; he was not interested in her mind and her soul, and *love* was to him simply a word which could be found in the dictionary. Her mind was arguing logically, but her heart continued to dwell on foolish hopes.

Alexa came to her senses with a start to discover that Revil had somehow manoeuvred her into the bedroom, and his hands were already tugging at the metal zip of her dress and sliding the thin straps off her shoulders. 'No!' she protested, dragging her mouth from his and clutching frantically at the cotton bodice, but one swift tug of his hand made her dress drop to the floor at her feet to leave her standing before him in her lacy underwear. 'Revil, please!' she begged anxiously, her cheeks flaming. 'Please don't!'

Revil was deaf to her pleas. His mouth claimed hers

once again, drugging her mind, and his hands gently stroked her heated body with a sensual expertise until her resistance crumbled to leave her trembling and pliant beneath his touch. Her flimsy underwear had become an annoying barrier between them which he removed in between sensually arousing kisses and caresses, and she was beyond caring when he lowered her on to the bed to slip off her sandals. His eyes were strangely dark and glazed with desire in the bedside light when he removed his shirt to expose his muscled, hair-roughened chest, but, when his hands went to the belt at his waist, her mind was invaded with a breath of sanity.

She had to get away from him before it was too late, but Revil displayed the uncanny ability to gauge the frantic thoughts racing through her mind. He was beside her in an instant, preventing her escape by holding her down effortlessly with one hand while he discarded the remainder of his clothes with the other. Anger seemed to mingle with desire in his smouldering eyes, and she cringed inwardly with embarrassment when his heated glance trailed over her naked body.

'God, Alexa, you're so very beautiful,' he groaned savagely, his fiery glance lingering on her smooth, shapely thighs, her flat stomach, and the soft swell of her small breasts with their hardened peaks. 'You're the most beautiful woman I've ever seen, and you're mine for the taking.'

'*No!*' she protested, the word passing her lips on a jerky, anguished breath.

'*Yes*, Alexa,' he contradicted her harshly, holding her down with one hand while he discarded the rest of his clothes. 'You will be lying if you deny that you want me. I can see it in your eyes, and I can feel it when I touch your lovely body.'

His hands were in her hair, his fingers tightening on the silvery strands as he lowered his head and crushed her mouth beneath his with a passionate urgency before he sought the swell of her breast, and she couldn't suppress the groan of pleasure that passed her lips when his warm, moist mouth closed over her hardened nipple.

It was true, she wanted him, and she couldn't deny it to herself. The aching need to be possessed was like an inextinguishable fire spreading throughout her body, and it consumed her, leaving her mindless. She was unaware that she was clinging to him feverishly, her hands moving convulsively against his muscled back, and her nails scraping his damp skin as her excitement mounted. Her sensitised flesh responded wildly beneath the arousing intimacy of his stroking fingers, and she had no control over her quivering body when it arched invitingly towards his.

'Tell me you want me!' he demanded in a husky voice as he parted her thighs and shifted his heated, aroused body over hers. 'Tell me you want me, Alexa! Show me!'

What am I doing? she asked herself, her hands stilling against his shoulders, and a painful coldness clutching at her insides as she came to her senses.

'Revil!' she gasped, writhing frantically beneath him to escape his invasion. 'I can't . . . please . . . I didn't want it to go this far, and I—I can't let you do this to me!'

'What do you mean, you can't let me do this to you?' Revil growled against her throat, his voice understandably harsh and angry, and she flinched as it grated across her raw, exposed nerves. 'Dammit, Alexa, I can't stop now!'

'You've got to! Please, Revil, you've got to . . . for your own sake as well as mine!'

Her face was flushed with the effort to push him away,

and he raised his head at that moment to see the blind panic in her eyes.

'Dammit, it isn't possible!' He shuddered with the supreme effort it took to leash his desire, and a look of disbelief invaded the banked-down fire in his eyes. 'You're scared out of your wits!'

Her lips quivered and tears filled her eyes. 'Revil, I'm sorry. It's all my fault.'

'My God, you were right when you said I wouldn't recognise the truth if it was staring me in the face!' he exclaimed harshly, thrusting himself away from her, and running a shaky hand through his hair when he sat on the edge of the bed. 'You're a virgin, aren't you.'

It was a statement, not a query, and she was too choked to do anything but nod in reply when he turned his head to look at her over his shoulder.

'My God!' he said again, and she was amazed to see pain and guilt in the smoke-grey glance that held hers. 'You're a virgin!'

His laugh was harsh with a sting of self-mockery in its depths as he got up to put on his clothes, and it felt as if a bucket of iced water had been poured over her, killing every scrap of desire which had still lingered with an aching sweetness inside her.

She sat up abruptly, swinging her legs off the side of the bed, and turning her back on him while she wrapped her arms about her shivering body. 'I'm sorry you had to find out this way.'

'*You're* sorry!' His voice was bitingly cold, and it stabbed her to the core. 'How the hell do you think *I* feel? *Dammit*, Alexa, I've known for some time that you're not the kind of woman my sister led me to believe you were, but there was a stubborn part of me that wouldn't accept the fact that both Wilma and James had lied to me, and now I have proof of it!'

'You've accused me before of lying to you,' she said warily without turning. 'How can you be sure I haven't lied to you now?'

'No, Alexa, you haven't lied to me, and don't try to cushion the pain for me.' She ought to have felt overjoyed, but the weariness in his deep, beautiful voice made her want to weep for him. 'I suggest you get dressed.'

Her clothes were flung on to the bed beside her, and her face flamed with embarrassment, but the blood receded from her cheeks the next instant to leave her pale and mercifully numb. She put on her clothes, neither knowing nor caring whether he was watching her, but she paused at the door and turned to see him standing in front of the window and staring into the darkness with his shoulders hunched and his clenched fists resting on the windowsill.

The life seemed to flow back into her body, and with it came the pain and the anguish of knowing that Revil could never love her, but she did not dwell on her own misery. Her compassionate heart was aching instead for Revil. She wanted to take him in her arms and comfort him, but she dared not, and her eyes filled with tears of helplessness.

'Revil, I——'

'Please go.' He interrupted the apology which had once again spilled from her lips, and his cold, abrupt voice placed a chasm between them which she feared might never be breached. 'I need time to think.'

She stared at him through a film of tears, taking in every wavery detail of his appearance as if it would have to last her a lifetime, then she left his bungalow and walked blindly into the night with a leaden feeling in her breast.

Alexa entered her own bungalow a short while later

without knowing how she had found her way there. She changed into her cool cotton nightie and got into bed to lie staring into the darkness. What was Revil doing? What was he thinking? Did he hate her for the part she had played in the destruction of his faith in his sister?

Her throat ached, and hot tears spilled from her dark lashes to scald her cheeks. She tried to check them, but without success, and she finally turned her face into her pillow to sob bitterly until she felt drained and empty, and too exhausted to do anything but sleep.

The following morning, when she left her bungalow, she heard a plane taking off, and she paused outside her door for a moment to watch it climbing into the cloud-flecked sky. It was taking Revil back to Johannesburg and, she feared, out of her life, and a dead weight settled in her chest, to linger there for the rest of her stay at the game park.

CHAPTER TEN

THE weather in Johannesburg was uncomfortably cold after the warm climate of the northern Transvaal, but the last few days at Izilwane had become an extended nightmare from which Alexa had been glad to escape. A week passed with not a word from Revil, and she had spent most of her time at Madame Véronique's studio, working her way listlessly through a series of exercises to keep her body supple. She had listened to Madame discussing André Dacre's show of summer fashions, but her mind had adopted a negative attitude towards it.

Every time the telephone rang in her flat or in Madame's studio she expected it to be Revil, but the voice at the other end of the line had never been his. Where was Revil? What was he doing, and what was he thinking? Dear God, perhaps it was best that she didn't know! And perhaps she ought to resign herself to the growing conviction that Revil's interest in her had waned now that he knew she was innocent of the vile accusations Wilma and her late husband had made.

On the Monday evening, ten days after Alexa's return from Izilwane, she answered the ring of her doorbell to find Madame Véronique standing on her doorstep, and Alexa stared at her in startled surprise.

'May I come in, Alexa, or am I not welcome this evening?' Madame smiled, and Alexa came swiftly to her senses.

'Of course, Madame, you know you're always welcome.' She stood aside to let the older woman in, and she closed the door, shutting out the cold night air before she led the way into the lounge. 'Could I offer you a cup of tea?'

'Later perhaps,' said Madame Véronique, her face grave when they sat facing each other in Alexa's small lounge. 'I am not going to beat about the bush, as you say. I want to know what is wrong.'

'Wrong?' Alexa's nerves jarred violently as if she had become a musical instrument on which Madame had struck a wrong chord, and her body grew taut as an incredible tension built up within her. 'Nothing is wrong, Madame.'

'Ah, *chérie*, I am not a fool,' Madame announced gravely. 'I have known for some time now that all is not well with you, but since your return from Izilwane it has been more noticeable.' Her brown eyes softened with that familiar warmth and concern when Alexa hesitated. 'I do not have to tell you that you can trust me, *chérie*.'

Alexa stared at Madame Véronique, but it was Revil's face she was seeing, his tanned, good-looking features harsh with incredulous disbelief, and pain and guilt mingling with the leashed passion which had still smouldered in his eyes. It was as if a door in her mind had slammed shut that night at Izilwane, capturing that image of Revil and refusing to set it free, but the door had suddenly been ripped from its hinges. Something snapped inside her, and she burst into tears to sob brokenly into her hands.

'*Mon Dieu*!' Madame Véronique exclaimed, reverting to her native tongue in her astonishment. 'I have never seen anyone weep such terrible tears. Tell me what it is, *chérie*. I insist!'

Embarrassed by her sudden display of emotion in front of Madame Véronique, Alexa made a strenuous effort to control herself and, fumbling in the pocket of her skirt for her handkerchief, she dabbed frantically, but unsuccessfully at tears which persisted in flowing down her pale cheeks. 'Forgive me, Madame, but I—I can't talk about it.'

Madame leaned forward in her chair, her dark eyes observing Alexa intently. 'Only a man could make a woman weep such bitter tears. Is it Revil Bradstone?'

Alexa's red-rimmed, puffy eyes registered surprise, and her lips were quivering as she stared at the elegantly dressed woman seated close to her. 'How—how did you know, Madame?' she whispered.

'I have been observing you closely, and I have seen the way you look at him,' Madame explained quietly. 'You are in love with him, *chérie*.'

Alexa's heart lurched uncomfortably. If Madame Véronique had guessed her feelings, then it was possible Revil might have done the same. Was that why she had not heard from him since her return from Izilwane?

'I will not insist that you tell me what happened between Revil Bradstone and yourself, *petite amie*, but I do not like to see you so distraught,' Madame's faintly accented voice intruded on Alexa's tormented thoughts.

Distraught! That word was too mild to describe the way she was feeling, Alexa thought, a hint of hysteria in the smile which came and went on her quivering lips. She had been foolish enough to fall in love with a man who could never love her in return, a man who had acquainted himself with her because of that desire for revenge which now no longer existed, but all she wanted at that moment was to get as far away from him as she possibly could. She needed time to think, and time to decide what to do about the desolate future which faced her.

The tears flowed fast once again. She could not decide whether her tears were for herself or for Revil, but it made no difference, and Madame made no attempt to comfort or rebuke her. 'Tears are good for the soul,' she had once told Alexa, and Alexa's soul was like a vacuum inside her when she finally wiped away her tears with her soggy handkerchief.

'I'm sorry, Madame,' she apologised, her voice an exhausted whisper.

'I think we will both have that cup of tea now, but stay where you are,' Madame instructed authoritatively as she rose from her chair. 'I shall make myself at home in your kitchen.'

'Madame?' Alexa felt numb with misery, and her face was white and pinched as she sat staring helplessly up at the older woman. 'I'd like to go away for a while, if I may, but I don't know where to go to, and I feel so——'

Madame Véronique smiled gently and gestured her to silence. 'Leave everything to me, Alexa.'

The Wild Coast lived up to its name; it was a wild and often rugged terrain, but it was beautiful in its own way, and the weather was surprisingly warm for August. Alexa had been on several long walks during her first week at the holiday hotel owned by close friends of Madame Véronique. She had followed the mapped-out trails through the bush where the guava trees grew wild among the many other indigenous flowering trees, but she had spent most of her time walking aimlessly along the beach, or sitting on a sand dune while she watched the tide come in and go out.

Alexa sighed deeply as she walked along the lonely stretch of sand in the late afternoon sun with the sea breeze whipping her cotton frock about her shapely legs. Paradise Cove, the holiday hotel was called, and it *was* Paradise to Alexa. She had felt oddly safe from the moment Madame Véronique had taken charge of her immediate future two weeks ago, and it was Madame who had made all the necessary arrangements. Alexa simply had to pack a bag and get herself on to the bus which had taken her to Umtata in the Transkei where Madame's friends, a kindly Belgian couple, had met her to take her the rest of the way by car along bumpy gravel roads. At the end of her journey Alexa had found Paradise, but it had taken almost two weeks in these peaceful surroundings before Alexa was able to say with honesty that she had begun to think and feel normally.

No one had intruded on her privacy. She had come and gone at will from her small thatched *rondavel*, and the clean, fresh sea air had given her an appetite, the result of which she was beginning to feel on her clothes.

At first she had tried not to think of Revil. It had been too painful and too humiliating. When she thought of him now, it was in anger, a slow, simmering anger which she could not explain, and which she hoped would finally abate to leave her with absolutely no feeling for him at all.

A helicopter came in low over the trees before it circled and landed somewhere near the hotel. The sound of its rotor blades disturbed the perfect silence of Paradise Cove, but Alexa paid little attention to it. She had to start thinking about her future, but it was a subject she still wanted to shy away from. Her future was like a barren stretch of land spread out ahead of her, with no promise of a tomorrow. Without Revil there would be no tomorrow for her to look forward to.

Alexa sighed heavily, and lowered herself on to the sand. Would she ever stop reaching for that star which could never be hers, she wondered, pulling her knees up under her chin, and drawing patterns idly in the sand with a smooth, bleached stick which had been washed up on the beach. Tomorrow. The word had a hollow sound to it which echoed painfully through her tortured mind.

She would think about the future tomorrow.

The evenings were cool, and Alexa wore her blue, long-sleeved woollen dress to dinner that evening to give her sufficient warmth. She did not pin her hair up, but left it free as she had done since her arrival at Paradise Cove, and it added a slight touch of youthful sophistication to her elegant appearance.

The dining-room was still comparatively empty when Alexa walked in and seated herself at her usual table beside the window overlooking the beach in the distance. She had felt calm and relaxed when she ordered the soup, but everything inside her seemed to grind to a frightening halt when she looked up a few minutes later to see Revil standing beside her table. His face looked grim, his eyes sunken and tired, but nothing registered for a moment except that terrible tension building up inside her once her heart and lungs had resumed their normal function.

What was he doing here? What did he want?

'May I join you?' he asked, gesturing towards the empty chair at her table.

'What are you doing here?' she demanded coldly, taking in his grey slacks, light-weight blue jacket, and white open-necked shirt. He looked devastating, but she was determined not to give in to the potency of his masculine appeal.

'I came to see you.' His hand touched the back of the chair, pulling it out slightly from beneath the table. 'May I, Alexa?'

'I can't stop you, can I?' she smiled cynically.

His mouth tightened, but he did not let her cynical remark prevent him from joining her at her table. The black-skinned waitress, in her traditional Xhosa dress, came to take his order and, when she left, he leaned slightly towards Alexa and pinned her to her chair with his smoky glance.

'I came here to talk to you, and what I have to tell you is extremely important. To me, at any rate,' he added grimly. 'If you would grant me just five minutes of your time after dinner this evening, then I'll have my say, and leave, if that's what you want.'

'I suppose Madame Véronique told you where I was,' she said, ignoring his statement. Or had it been a plea?

'Yes, she did, but after a great deal of persuasion, I might add,' he smiled grimly, but Alexa's expression remained stony.

'How did you get here?'

'I took a flight from Jan Smuts to Durban, and I managed to hire a helicopter from there.'

That explained the helicopter she had seen arriving late that afternoon, but she was still ignorant of the reason he had resorted to such extravagance to get in touch with her. 'I can't think of anything you have to say which might interest me.'

'Five minutes, Alexa,' he pleaded with that odd, grim urgency she had never seen before. 'Please?'

Alexa hesitated. Was this a new way of baiting yet another hook to trap her? Five minutes. That was all he had asked for, and then he would leave. Could she take that chance?

'Very well,' she agreed, and his features relaxed slightly as if he had feared she might refuse him.

No, her mind jeered cynically. Revil was not afraid of anything. He was always in complete control.

They made no attempt at conversation while they ate their meal and, when they left the table, Revil followed her in silence from the main building to her *rondavel*, which consisted of a bedroom with two single beds and a bathroom. She didn't particularly like the idea of taking him there, but it was the only place where they could talk privately, she decided, when she unlocked the door and went in ahead of him to switch on the light. Revil followed her inside and closed the door, shutting out the cool night air, and Alexa felt her nerves start to quiver with a growing tension at being alone with him like this.

'All right, Revil,' she said, adopting a cool, business-like attitude as she flung her purse on to the dressing-table and turned rigidly to face him. 'You have the five minutes you asked for.'

Her travelling alarm clock on the bedside cupboard ticked away the seconds while he stood with his hands thrust into his pockets, and his frowning glance lowered to the serviceable brown carpet beneath his expensive shoes.

'Both Carol and Byron tried to warn me with their infernal quotations that I was setting a trap for myself, but I wouldn't listen to them.' He raised his glance, and there was a strangely haunted look in the eyes that met hers. 'I love you, Alexa.'

She drew a strangled breath. He had delivered a savage and unexpected blow to her most vulnerable spot . . . her heart . . . and the blood drained from her face to leave her ashen.

'Of all the things you've said to hurt me, that is—is the cruellest, the most despicable——' She could not go on and, blinded by tears, she stormed across the room and flung open the door. 'Get out!'

'Not so fast!' Revil jerked the door out of her grasp and slammed it shut. 'You said you'd give me five minutes of your time, and I insist on having my say before I leave.'

'You have no right to insist on anything!' she almost shouted at him, the sheen of tears still in her eyes when they blazed up into his at the thought of all the suffering she had been forced to endure.

'Alexa...' His hands reached out to her, but she backed away from him sharply, and he dropped his hands to his sides again. For the first time she saw him looking awkward and unsure of himself, but the smoky gaze that met hers was steady and grave. 'For three years I believed every word Wilma had told me because I had never known her to lie to me before. I was angry, and I swore that I'd make you pay if we ever met again, but I'm sure I'm not the first person to discover that things don't always work out as planned. You didn't look like the type of woman I believed you to be, and you didn't act that way. I wanted to despise you, but instead I found myself wanting you as I've never wanted a woman before, and that made me furious. I told myself that you were putting on an act to deceive me, and I acted accordingly, but I knew somehow that you were sincere.'

Alexa was wary of him, but her anger seemed to drain away from her, and she sat down heavily on the bed behind her when her legs started to shake beneath her. 'I imagine that was when you began to suspect that Wilma had lied to you.'

'My suspicions were aroused that very first day when you came to my office. Your loyalty and concern for Madame Véronique struck the first chord of doubt in my mind, but I behaved like a swine, and I don't blame you for continuing to believe that I had some sadistic plan in mind for you.' His features wore a grim, tortured expression when he sat down facing her on the other bed, and his knees were so close to hers that they brushed against the skirt of her dress. 'Do you know what it's like to be torn between your love for one person and your loyalty to another? God help me, Alexa, but I've been going through a hell of my own making, and I made you suffer just as much.'

Alexa felt confused and bewildered. She wanted to reach out to him with her warm, spontaneous heart, but a part of her remained wary of grasping at something which might turn to dust in her hands. 'Why didn't you contact me again after that night at Izilwane when you——'

'When I had my suspicions confirmed once and for all that you were still a virgin?' he filled in for her with that haunted look back in his eyes when he reached across the space between them to grip her hands tightly. 'I despised myself for allowing my usually sound judgment to be clouded by my sister's lies, and I despised myself for doubting you, but it was the thought of my disreputable behaviour that kept me away from you. I was convinced that you would never want to see me again.'

'What made you change your mind about that?'

'My need to be with you became stronger than my sense of shame.' He smiled faintly as if the memory amused him. 'When I couldn't find you I contacted Madame Véronique, and I don't mind telling you that before she gave me your address she gave me a lecture which I doubt if I shall ever forget.' His expression sobered, and he slowly raised her hands to his lips. 'I love you, and I need you, Alexa. Are you going to send me away, my darling?'

My darling! Alexa's heart turned over in her breast at what she saw in his eyes, and she felt as if she had been given a rare and precious gift which she knew she would cherish for the rest of her life. She could not suppress that sweet, singing joy that tingled through her veins like warm, intoxicating wine, and her wariness and doubts fell from her like a cloak with the knowledge that Revil loved her and needed her. It was like a soothing balm, washing away the the memory of all the times she had been hurt, and taking with it the pain and anguish she had suffered.

'How can I send you away now that I know you love me and need me?' she asked tremulously.

Her heart had been there in her eyes for him to see, but that touching and unfamiliar uncertainty was still in the smoky gaze that held hers. 'I know I can make you want me physically, but do you think there's a chance that you might learn to care for me in the way I care for you?'

'Oh, Revil!' she whispered shakily, sliding off the bed to kneel between his knees, and she slipped her hands inside his jacket to wrap her arms about his waist as she buried her face against his chest. 'I love you! I love you so much it *hurts*!'

His arms were hard about her, crushing her against him as if he never wanted to let her go, and quite some time elapsed before he tilted her face up to his and kissed her with a lingering tenderness that touched her heart in a way that nothing had ever done before.

'You and I have some unfinished business to attend to,' he said at length, and his statement as well as that hint of anger in his eyes had a sobering effect on Alexa. 'I want you with me when I confront Wilma.'

'Have you seen her since her return from Greece?' she asked cautiously, treading on ground which she still felt was uncertain.

'I've spoken to her very briefly on the telephone.'

Alexa avoided his eyes as she extricated herself gently from his arms to seat herself on the bed beside him. 'I don't suppose you have given her any indication that you are aware she lied to you.'

'No, I haven't.' Out of the corner of her eyes she could see his mouth tightening ominously. 'The art of surprise often has the desired effect, and if she doesn't tell the truth this time I'll shake it out of her.'

'Oh, Revil . . .' she whispered brokenly, knowing in her heart that this confrontation with Wilma Henderson was going to be a painful ordeal for him as well as his sister, and her vision blurred.

'Tears?' he questioned her, lowering his head to brush them away with his lips. 'What are these tears for?'

'Oh, it's nothing,' she laughed shakily. 'I cry sometimes for the oddest reasons.'

His arm went about her, and his warm, possessive and demanding mouth shifted over hers. Her pulse quickened, and her senses sharpened on a note of desire as she returned his kisses with a hunger that rose like a tide inside her. She felt him alter his position slightly to ease her back against the pillows, and he held her a prisoner on the bed with the weight of his body. Her hand had somehow found its way inside his shirt to assuage that longing to feel his warm skin against her palm, and she felt the tremors of desire coursing through his body.

'Will you fly back to Johannesburg with me tomorrow?' he asked against her throbbing, eager lips.

'Yes, if that's what you want.'

'I want, but I'm beginning to want so much more,' he groaned, moving his body against hers and making her intoxicatingly aware of his heated desire. 'Are you going to let me stay with you tonight?'

Her hand stilled its exploration of his chest. She wanted to say *yes*, but her mind warned against it. He had said that he loved and needed her, but he had not given her an indication of what kind of future they would have together. She knew not to expect an offer of marriage from this man, but she needed time to decide whether she could accept the kind of relationship he had in mind, and she could not give herself to him while there was still that tiny shadow of doubt in her mind.

'No,' she said softly, sliding her hand up along his strong, sun-browned throat, and tracing the line of his jaw with tender fingers. 'I love you, Revil, but I—I'd prefer to wait for a more appropriate time and place,' she lied uncomfortably. 'Would you mind very much waiting?'

He drew back, frowning slightly, but with that smoky fire of desire still lingering in his eyes. 'You're allowing our meeting with Wilma to cast a shadow over this moment, but I dare say it won't kill me to wait, if that's what you want.' He kissed her hard on the mouth and got up, drawing her to her feet with him. 'I'll see you in the morning. And don't run away again, will you?'

'I'll be here,' she promised, drawing his head down to kiss him lightly on the lips. 'Goodnight, Revil.'

His chest heaved against her, and he pulled her into his arms to kiss her hard and satisfyingly on the mouth before he left, but his presence seemed to linger in the *rondavel* with her while she undressed and got into bed. It felt as if she were moving in a dream, but if this was a dream, then . . . please God . . . she prayed that it would never end.

The helicopter flight from Paradise Cove to Durban was an enjoyable experience, and she shouldn't have been surprised when she saw Revil produce a ticket made out in her name for the flight back to Johannesburg. He had not been entirely sure of his success, but he was not going to take the chance of being caught unprepared, he explained when he found her looking at him with a mixture of curiosity and amusement.

He looked rested and relaxed, and that haggard, grim look had almost gone from his features. He held her hand during the flight from Durban to Johannesburg, and he

kissed her several times as if he took a devilish delight in
seeing her blush at the thought that they were being
observed by the other passengers, but Alexa was simply
too happy be rebuke him.

Revil had left his Jaguar parked at Jan Smuts airport,
and Alexa turned slightly in her seat to face him when
they drove away from the airport. 'I presume your sister
isn't expecting us.'

'No, she isn't.'

'Wouldn't it be kinder for you to speak to her alone?'
Alexa asked tentatively, and his stern expression
softened when he glanced at her briefly.

'You're so gentle and caring, Alexa, and I think that's
one of the reasons why I love you so much,' he said
throatily, taking her hand and placing it on his hard
thigh. 'You ought to hate Wilma for accusing you so
unjustly, and yet you can still find it in your heart to feel
concern for her.'

'I don't hate your sister,' Alexa explained after giving
the matter a moment of thought. 'I think she must have
had a very good reason for lying to you.'

'What reason could she have had to lie to me?' he
demanded incredulously.

'Perhaps she had cause to fear your anger if you knew
the truth,' she reasoned with him, recalling what Byron
Rockford had said about his suspicion that Wilma was
afraid of Revil.

Revil frowned at the road ahead of them without
responding to her statement, and Alexa felt the tension
in him as if it were her own.

Wilma Henderson lived in a magnificent old house set
in a spacious, well-kept garden, and Alexa's heart was
beating nervously against her ribs when they waited in
the modernly furnished living-room while the maid
went upstairs to tell Revil's sister that she had visitors.

They didn't speak while they waited, but the look on Revil's face made her tremble inwardly in sympathy with his sister.

The sound of footsteps in the hall made them glance quickly at each other, and then Wilma Henderson came into the living-room. She was exactly as Alexa had remembered her. She was tall, dark and slender, and there was a striking resemblance between Revil and his sister when they embraced each other casually, except that Wilma's eyes were an attractive grey-green.

'Revil, how nice to see you, I——'

Wilma's voice faded into silence when her glance met Alexa's across the room, and Revil turned with a tight smile about his mouth. 'You remember Alexa Drew, don't you?'

Wilma Henderson went pale beneath the tan she had acquired on the Greek Islands. 'Yes, I—I remember her very well.'

'Perhaps your memory is also good enough to recall the reason for your unfounded accusations against her,' Revil announced, and his sister had the look of someone who had had a charged explosive device dropped in her lap.

Byron Rockford had been right after all, Alexa realised when she looked into Wilma's grey-green eyes. She was afraid of Revil.

'Shall we sit down?' There was a distinct tremor in Wilma's hands when she gestured towards the comfortably padded, expensively upholstered chairs. 'I dare say I owe you an explanation.'

'I should damn well think you do!' Revil exploded harshly when they had seated themselves. 'And it had better be a good one!'

Wilma's face had gone almost as white as the lacy collar of her blouse, and shame and remorse mingled with the fear in her eyes. 'You have every right to be angry with me, but perhaps when I've explained——'

'That's what we're waiting for!' Revil interrupted his sister unkindly, and Alexa felt sorry for Wilma when she saw her wring her hands nervously in her lap.

'It's a long story, but I'll do my best to make it as brief as possible,' Wilma began, her voice suddenly fraught with bitterness. 'You weren't too keen on the idea that I should marry James. You said he wasn't the right man for me, but I wouldn't listen to you. We weren't married very long when I discovered my mistake, but I was too proud to admit it, and while I remained silent, James went ahead and succeeded in convincing you that he was a model husband. He was so good at convincing you that he was making me the happiest woman that walked the earth, that you set him up in a business of his own, but the truth was that he could never leave anything in a skirt alone. He assaulted me brutally one night when I dared to accuse him of being unfaithful to me, and as a result I lost the child I was carrying. When I wanted to leave him he threatened to sue me for every cent of my inheritance, so I decided to use whatever method, foul or otherwise, I could to acquire the necessary evidence for a divorce, but that night, when I found Alexa in his hotel bedroom, I panicked. *You* were there, I was afraid of what you might do, and I lied about what I saw.'

Revil's hands clenched into fists on the arms of the chair and a frightening whiteness settled about his tight mouth.

'I stupidly covered up for James in front of you, and I'm not very proud of what I did.' Wilma's confession added fuel to the explosive atmosphere in the living-room. 'James played along with me, but he was scared. He knew that, if I had Alexa called in as a witness, there would be sufficient evidence for me to divorce him, and he was aware that I had every intention of gaining my freedom. He also knew that he would lose everything he had acquired during our marriage when you discovered the truth, and he was panicking. He staged a dramatic act one evening. He said he couldn't live without me, and he threatened to kill himself if I went ahead with the divorce. He raised a gun to his head, but I laughed at him because I thought it wasn't loaded, and I firmly believe James thought so too, but there was one cartridge left in the magazine.' She paused briefly, and swallowed nervously before she continued. 'Alexa told the truth, Revil. James lured her up to his room on the pretext that he was ill. He had used that old trick on me often enough, and with success, because sex was the only thing we still had in common, but his tactics didn't work on Alexa. She was fighting him off like the very devil when I walked into that room.'

'My God!' Revil exploded hoarsely into the strained silence, his ashen face distorted with a frightening fury. 'I could thrash you for the unnecessary suffering your lies caused!'

'I think I'd like to take a walk through the garden, if you don't mind,' Alexa excused herself quietly when she began to feel like an intruder, and no one tried to stop her when she stepped outside through the french windows to take a stroll in the garden while brother and sister held their post mortem in private.

She found a bench in a shaded part of the sunlit garden, and sat down rather tiredly. It was such a beautiful day. The sun was shining, and the birds were singing in the trees, but in Alexa's heart there were shadowy, pain-filled corners. The mind was a cruel instrument. It conjured up those moments of pain and suffering which belonged in the past, and they were as fresh as if they had happened the day before.

She closed her eyes against the tears that threatened, and when she opened them some minutes later she saw Revil lowering himself on to the bench beside her.

'Alexa?' His eyes were dark with the pain she had felt when he pulled her into his arms and buried his face against her throat. 'I can't ask you to forgive me for ever doubting you, because I can't forgive myself, but I'll make it up to you. I swear I'll make it up to you.'

'No, my darling,' she smiled through her tears as she framed his face between her hands. 'Love me, just love me.'

An oddly strangled sound passed his lips, and then his mouth was ravaging hers as if he wished, in that way, to obliterate the memory of everything that had gone before.

'Let's get away from here.' He voiced her own desire when he gave her an opportunity to draw breath, and she nodded her approval of his suggestion without speaking.

Revil took her to his penthouse, and the pencil sketch Megan had made of her was the first thing she noticed when she entered the lounge. The sketch was hanging against the wall where it could be seen from almost every chair in the room, and this time she had no doubts about why it was there.

They made themselves a cup of tea in Revil's kitchen, and they drank it out on the sunny roof garden with its potted shrubs and flower boxes filled with geraniums which would bloom in spring. They talked for some time, but Alexa sensed an undercurrent of something which left her tense and nervous. It eventually drove her to her feet to stand looking over the high wall surrounding the roof garden, and she stared out across the city without actually seeing anything.

'There are certain things which still have to be said

between us, but I have a feeling you would rather they remained unsaid,' he observed with a hint of the old mockery in his voice as he came up behind her.

'Some things are better left unsaid,' she admitted, but she knew that it would be childish of her to evade the issue when there was still so much she did not understand. 'What plans did you have in mind for me after that assignment at Izilwane?' she asked, not daring to look at him while she steeled herself for his reply.

'I had plans to help you finance your own modelling agency. I also intended asking you to live with me, and that's an offer which still stands.'

Alexa was not sure what she had expected, but his words were like a knife edge scraping across raw, tender nerves, and she turned to face him, hiding her pain behind that cool mask she had thought she would never need to wear in his presence again.

'You want me to live with you?' she heard herself asking as if she needed his statement confirmed.

'Would you?'

Alexa hesitated, shivering inwardly as the sun dipped behind a cloud. Would she live with him? *Could* she? she asked herself. To live with him would be preferable to having no part of him at all, she argued with herself, but ... what would happen afterwards? Would she be able to live with herself knowing that she had lived with a man who had cast her aside when he no longer loved and needed her? Would she still have her self-respect?

'For how long would you want me to live with you? A month? Two months? A year, perhaps?' she asked, no longer capable of hiding the bitterness of her pain and disappointment.

'I was thinking in terms of a lifetime,' he said, his fingers biting into her waist as if he wished to punish her for doubting him, and his mouth twisted into a faintly mocking smile as he drew her into his arms. 'I could make the necessary arrangements this afternoon and we could be married tomorrow, if you'll have me.'

The painful beat of her heart quickened to a joyous peak, but a part of her was too stunned to believe what he had said.

'You want to marry me?' she asked huskily, almost choking on the words, and the mockery in his smile faded.

'The time for playing games is in the past. You're the woman I want to spend the rest of my life with, and the woman I want to have my children with.' His fingers bit into her waist with a certain urgency. 'Will you marry me, Alexa? Will you be the mother of my children?'

Alexa was too choked to speak for a moment. She ought not to allow him an easy victory after those few agonising seconds she had been forced to endure, but when she looked up into his smoke-grey eyes she knew that this was not the time to tease. He was allowing her to see into his heart, and the wonder of it made her want to cry.

'I'll marry you, Revil, and I'll have your children for you,' she whispered, her eyes moist with tears of happiness and a joy which was almost to great to bear. 'And it would suit me very nicely if you could arrange a quiet ceremony tomorrow rather than an elaborate affair with hordes of strangers looking in on something which ought to be private and intimate.'

'Alexa,' he groaned, his voice vibrant with emotion as he pulled her roughly back into his arms, and his eyes were smouldering with a tender passion that made her tremble. 'I love you, and God knows my life would become worthless without you.'

'Oh, Revil,' she sighed as his sensuous mouth descended to claim her eager lips in a tender, lingering kiss that made her ache for more.

His hands roamed her body, their arousing touch making the blood race through her veins at a mad pace, and she tugged at his shirt buttons, incapable of controlling her own feverish desire to touch him.

'I want you, Alexa,' Revil groaned against her mouth when her fingers strayed across his male nipples. 'Do we have to wait until tomorrow?'

'No,' she murmured, dizzy with desire, and his mouth shifted over hers once more with a demanding passion that lit an answering flame inside her.

She wanted him. Her body had recognised this need to be conquered by his long before her mind and her heart would acknowledge it, and Alexa returned his kisses with a growing hunger which seemed to leap from the depths of her soul.

The sun emerged at last from behind that stray cloud as Revil lifted her gently in his arms and carried her inside, and Alexa felt the warmth of it against her skin for a brief moment before they entered the penthouse, but the warmth of her love would linger inside her to shut out the past until yesterday became a memory which no longer had the power to rob her of a joyous tomorrow.

Harlequin Presents

Coming Next Month

Available in November wherever paperback books are sold, or through
Harlequin Reader Service:

In the U.S.
901 Fuhrmann Blvd.
P.O. Box 1397
Buffalo, N.Y. 14240-1397

In Canada
P.O. Box 603
Fort Erie, Ontario
L2A 5X3

Take 4 books & a surprise gift FREE

SPECIAL LIMITED-TIME OFFER

Mail to   **Harlequin Reader Service®**

In the U.S.
901 Fuhrmann Blvd.
P.O. Box 1867
Buffalo, N.Y. 14269-1867

In Canada
P.O. Box 609
Fort Erie, Ontario
L2A 5X3

YES!   Please send me 4 free Harlequin Temptation® novels and my free surprise gift. Then send me 4 brand-new novels every month as they come off the presses. Bill me at the low price of $2.24 each*—a 10% saving off the retail price. There are no shipping, handling or other hidden costs. There is no minimum number of books I must purchase. I can always return a shipment and cancel at any time. Even if I never buy another book from Harlequin, the 4 free novels and the surprise gift are mine to keep forever.   142 BPX BP7F

*Plus 49¢ postage and handling per shipment in Canada.

Name   (PLEASE PRINT)

Address   Apt. No.

City   State/Prov.   Zip/Postal Code

This offer is limited to one order per household and not valid to present subscribers. Price is subject to change.   DOHT-SUB-1C

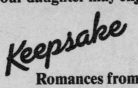